MI

Acknowledgements

This is dedicated to the dreamers whose passions take the driver's seats on their paths of destiny. Whose travels are undeterred by the traffic of challenges and the potholes of negativity and naysayers. For those who walk in the light of faith, hope, patience and perseverance when the path seems dark. For those who strive to live in the spirit of human excellence when popular culture promotes otherwise. For those who long for the inexhaustible breath of life that only their imaginations breathe into it. For those who judge their success outside the box for which the world has constructed and within the realm of the essence of peace and love that their heart and soul attains. For those whose friendship, love and support remained true when doubt cast over me like an unending dark cloud...I'm forever grateful.

And to the Creator of the Heavens and Earth for the vehicles which bore me; my parents, my rock and un-withered rose, Larry and Lizzie Bastain, whose love and life taught us kindness, compassion, humility and sacrifice and to appreciate and never buckle amidst struggle. For the seeds so borne me: Brooklynn, Mark, Myles, Hasan, Ruqaiyah and one borne from the heart, Cartiay. To my siblings who I derive the strength of my core, I'm still that lil dude. I always humbly stand your baby brother: Bobby, Geraldine, Reggie, Lawrence, Yolanda, Larry, Tim (RIP), and Nicole, who has traveled as many years as one of my own siblings. To my very

1

special cousin and friend, Pam, whose positive energy always inspires. To the in-laws whose love is as natural as family could be: Hasan, Janice, and Yamini. To my wife Yaphett, with love, appreciation and gratitude, who has traveled a storied road between cobblestone and pavement with great patience and sacrifice, the depth of the English language falls short in capturing my full sentiments in one paragraph, thanks for keeping it tight. To my comrade and brother, Amir Ben Solomon who embodies the fearless warrior spirit of a Kemetic King, whose wisdom I forever carry like a sword in battle. To the varied inspirations from the past and present who in letter and spirit helped shape this story...and the many others unnamed but know who you are...

Peace and blessings

Contents

CHAPTER I

The Beginning: From Kiener to Italy

The frenzied exit of the crowd gave indication that the verdict was coming forward. News reporters began their mad scramble to position themselves at the entrances to the court steps. For Mia, the anxiety and anticipation had become almost unbearable. The burden of the possible outcomes visibly weighed on her lovely, but worn, butterscotch skin. Eyes puffy from lack of sleep, an unending trail of tears had flowed from her cheeks without end since she'd left the airport that day; the day her world seemingly stopped on its axis. Tyson Penn, once the picture of great promise and potential, sat stoically at the defense table next to his attorney, Pauly, his confidence undaunted by the Herculean legal challenge before him. The suspense in the overflow room of onlookers was as thick as an owl's whisper as Judge Evans and District Attorney Stephenson conferred with each other, still visibly irritated at Pauly's refusal to accept the plea deal and his insistence on introducing new evidence. The trial was supposed to be an open and shut case. The District Attorney's office had offered a deal but they'd refused, and now the outcome lay at the mercy of the courts.

Ty previously insisted that Mia distance herself from him for the duration of the trial, yet his desire to be comforted by her presence still lingered as he coolly scanned the courtroom hoping that she had stubbornly defied his request. On the other hand, although ill-advised, Bri would not miss the opportunity to torment Ty with his mere presence. Mia sat inside her car, parked adjacent to the court house at Kiener Plaza, resisting the temptation to be too close. It was the very spot where she and Ty first intimated their passion for one another. Mia tapped her steering wheel, slowly dipping her head into a trance-like state to the Isley Brothers' *"Let Me Down Easy,"* wishing that she could speak with him. The prior weeks had seemed an eternity. She looked through the old text messages she'd saved from Ty, hoping to create enough spark to lift her from the dark challenge of the moment. Her efforts only elicited a deeper feeling of want, despair, love and loss, ultimately breaking the levees of her eyelids, springing forth a new flood of tears. Mia rushed to send one last text of encouragement in hopes of reaching him.... *"I AM AND WILL ALWAYS BE ETERNALLY YOURS, FROM ITALY TO KIENER,"* read the text. Moments later, upon receiving the unexpected text, Ty flashed a smile. For a fleeting but welcome moment, Ty felt a brief respite from the legal quicksand into which he hoped to avoid falling. The courtroom observers, media and family were puzzled; finding Ty's sanguine and jovial demeanor uncharacteristic of a courtroom moment. He seemed temporarily detached from the gravity of his situation, forgetting that his life lay in the balance, he texted a response back to Mia as the Judge deliberated his fate.... *"1-4-3, FOREVER FROM KIENER TO ITALY!"* Herself not expecting, yet welcoming, a response, lifted from her seat as if receiving an infusion of blood for her dying heart.

"In the case of the United States versus Tyson Sheldon Penn, has the jury reached a verdict?" Judge Evans asked of the jury. Juror #3, a gangly, elderly Caucasian woman stood with the paper that detailed the verdict in her hand.

"Yes, Your Honor. We find the defendant...." It was as if time stood still, as if someone had pushed pause and fast forward at the same time. Ty walked alongside Pauly, flashing a peace sign to

6

address the crowd. From a distance, Mia caught a glimpse of Ty placing his hand over his heart, smiling to signal to her his love. Mia received and reciprocated his gesture, driving away as she did after the first night they made love in the carriage at Kiener. Today, she knew, would be either the first day of her forever or the first day of their never.

Her heart's proposition was whittled down to one of two words...guilty, or innocent.

Tivoli was an Arcadian village situated twenty miles northeast of Rome. It was founded before what is now known as modern-Rome, and famous for its awe-inspiring gardens, fountains and impressive cascades fed from the Aniene River. The hillside slopes defined the pristine land, which was adorned with modest homes originally occupied by shepherds herding their flocks of sheep; the smell of olives permeated the air like heaven cast its incense. Tivoli was also known as the summer retreat of the wealthiest of Romans. The home of the Villa d' Este, a Renaissance-era place known for its colorful gardens and majestic fountains, a town that had preserved the classic traditions of Italy's past. Tivoli's cultural breast fed the world the sweet milk of the arts, literature and music; the likes of DaVinci, Raphael and Michelangelo, Dante', Petrarch, Boccaccio and Rossini. The local men commonly congregated in groups atop the broken blocks of concrete and undeveloped Renaissance-era street corners. The open air cafés ventilated the smell of pipe smoke as their women passed by, carting baskets of freshly picked olives.

It is here in Tivoli that the seeds of Mia Farone-Whitmore were planted deep in the fertile ground, and her roots firmly fixed as the century-old structures that speckle the Italian landscape. Lieutenant Davis Whitmore was an African-American Naval pilot, temporarily assigned to Sigonella, Italy from his quarters on the Naval carrier USS Bennington (CVS-20). The Bennington had been charting the waters of the Gulf of Tonkin shortly after the Korean War, in the fall of 1959. Lt. Whitmore was well-educated and culturally versed in history, arts and the sciences. This added depth to an already sizable attraction and curiosity of the local women; he completely defied stereotypes of Blacks they had come to commonly believe through folklore. Eventually, Lt. Whitmore was forced to make the decision to return back home to his native St. Louis, Missouri, or extend his military service. St. Louis was in the heart of the Midwest and a Mecca for southern transplants who sought to escape the rigid and oppressive racism of the Southern residue of the Confederacy that still lingered in the South.

St. Louis was a racially polarized city known for, as Davis explained…. a "town of shepherds herding meek flocks of sheep!" Davis used this reference towards what he perceived as the docile nature of African-Americans in expressing their angst against the social mistreatment, and economic and political marginalization of Blacks. Whitmore was of towering stature, a man whose baritone voice and streak of militancy mirrored that of famed actor and social activist, Paul Robeson.

He knew his chances were greater in Italy to enjoy a more esteemed social status. Davis's service in the military was made more appealing by Europe's social liberalism as it opened the doors to African-Americans that remained shut, if not locked, by the dark recesses of racism of the United States. After the end of his obligated military service, Davis ultimately chose to remain in Sigonella as an instructor for pilots on base. He became esteemed in the eyes of the locals, namely the Italian women who harbored a folklore-like curiosity and animal attraction to the rare Black men they encountered. This was, naturally, to the ire of men of Sigonella. Italians, especially in the countryside territories like Tivoli, were keen on preserving their social and cultural purity. It was here that he met a petite and beautiful, olive-skinned young woman from Tivoli. Her hair was like hand-woven silk from the Orient. Men commonly gathered where she'd frequent, chattering in whisper at the marvel of her beauty. She worked at the Naval Base's commissary where Davis would frequent and whose liking she had stoked.

It was Friday afternoon, the beginning of the weekend where the locals made it a ritual gathering at commissary where they'd often flirt to the approval of the young Italian women. Davis split through the crowd like a prizefighter. His confident baritone voice amplified over jeers of the locals as he calmly stood in front of her. "Good day!" Davis said. "I've come here often and yet I don't know your name?" he asked.

She answered in her soft, Italian accent. "Savita, Savita Farone!" she said, slowly batting her eyes. She gave no clear indication she had been taken in by his charm.

"Listen, I'm not trying to come on, as you seem to have your share." Davis said, referencing her consistent bevy of admirers. "But your beauty is simply stunning!" Davis told her, as he handed

9

Savita his money at the checkout. She smiled, taking note that Davis had waited in the crowded line only to check out a single pack of gum. She knew at this point that his occasional presence was no coincidence. Savita found Davis's approach humorous, flattering and cute. Davis wasn't aware of Savita's familiarity with him, as she had herself become smitten with his charm and stature. Each conversation between the two was like a sparkling drop into the bucket that would inevitably spill over. Davis had taken the liberty, or at that point, the risk, of securing tickets to Rossini's opera, *"The Barber of Seville."* Davis had observed, through Savita's conversation with her co-workers, her fondness for the arts and opera. In particular was her desire to attend this very popular work of Rossini's.

Nothing was ever happenstance with Davis, as he was meticulous in observing the smallest of details that escaped most. He was equipped with but a few prepared Italian words that he'd learned only moments before. Standing in the checkout line at Savita's register, he handed her the money for his purchase as usual. This time, though, it was wrapped around the tickets to Rossini's show. Davis pled with Savita to join him tonight, "Perfavore iscriversi' mi questa notta!" She was flattered at his obvious attempt to impress her, and moved that he was in tune with the one event that she had long expressed her desire to attend.

Fighting back her excitement, she calmly smiled and answered, "Si!"

Davis, a handsome, burly man with refined style and mannerisms, chartered a horse-drawn carriage, which was a common mode of transport on the inland of the old towns of Europe. He knew that the carriage garnered the romantic, old-town mystique of her native Tivoli. As Davis approached Savita's home, she watched through the crack of her window shade in nervous anticipation as the thoughts of words eluded the grasp of her tongue. The knock at the door caused her heart's beat to triple. Opening the door, she immediately found calm and the appropriate words. "Good evening…"

Before Savita could muster another word, he interjected…. "Wow!" His gaze locked upon the heavy, black silken brows that capped her dark, deep eyes, twinkling like black diamonds in a bed of white pearls.

Davis nearly forgot the stargazer lilies he brought for her, coincidentally her favorite. "Oh, are those for me or you just gonna hold them for yourself?" Savita asked jokingly.

"Oh yes! I was stuck for a moment," he said, slightly embarrassed.

After the evening cast an end to the performance, there was a feeling of a first time or a prom date, moments where the hope was of a night unending. Savita wanted to hold as much of the moment as possible, so they waited till the theatre had totally cleared. The awkwardness was thick as the stage curtains and as silent as the breaking dawn over the Italian hillside. Davis, confident, but ever-so-conscience to extend courtesy and respect, sat frozen, as the normally reserved Savita courageously placed her hand on his thigh, breaking the arctic thaw as she whispered… "Thank you!"

Emboldened by her move, Davis grabbed her hand, "Come on, let's go!" he said enthusiastically. Smiling and girlishly obliging, she followed him down the aisle, as he hopped on the stage, taking her through the stage curtains. This was Davis, confident, refined yet edgy and spontaneous. The rush of adrenaline was dizzying when they approached the door of Giovanni Marconi, who was famous throughout Europe and the lead actor of the show. "Excuse me sir, we enjoyed your show. Would you like to meet Savita Farone? She is unquestionably your biggest fan!" Davis said boldly, introducing Savita as she stood bewildered, amazed and completely enamored by Davis's brazen spontaneity, captivated by the lengths of his willingness to put a smile on her face.

The night was capped by a rather conservative flare as Davis, the ever-consummate gentleman, escorted Savita to her door after a long. It was a lovely stroll, one they both reluctantly wanted to end as the desire to embrace one another had just begun to peak. Before the night cast its shadow over the evening, Davis grabbed the lower cusp of her hands, taking them on a detour to his lips, gently kissing her fingers "Buona serra!" he said, as he walked backwards, locking in on her smile. The smile spoke of her longing for his continued presence. This night would forever make an imprint on them both.

Over the next few months they spent countless days and hours talking on the phone along the banks of the waterway. They developed a comfort far removed from the awkwardness of their first meeting. For many, the excitement of the newness of love would have long waned; for Davis and Savita, those moments never seemed to come. One morning Davis set out making his normal rounds to the commissary to visit Savita, but to his surprise and concern, she was not at work. As he turned to leave, the manager stopped Davis and told him Savita had an emergency that begged her absence. After hearing this, Davis hurried himself over to Savita's, finding her in tears when she opened the door. "Baby, what's wrong?"

Holding her head in the throne of his chest, he listened as she wailed uncontrollably, telling him in an inaudible voice, "My mother…she's not well, they've hospitalized her!" Added to her distress was her inability to afford the trip to Tivoli from Sigonella.

Davis didn't fully understand the depths of her distress, but attempted to ease her pain struck a comforting cord. "I can arrange our travel through Military Airlift Command. We can be there in less than two hours!" he said. Military Airlift Command, commonly known as MAC, flights were free or dramatically reduced flights that were made available to military personnel or their spouses. Davis knew this would take some string-pulling because Savita was not his spouse. What registered most with Savita, though, was the one word that provided the comfort she needed. It was the word that pulled her up from the depths of distress… "*We!*" It pierced the once impermeable chamber of her heart, evidence of just how close they had become. Dumbfounded and stricken mute, Savita wrapped her arms around Davis's waist, holding him closely and firmly. It was in this moment that she believed, for the first time, she was not alone.

The next flight from Sigonella was leaving in two hours for Rome, which was almost thirty miles southwest of Tivoli, so they rushed off to the airport. The physical closeness they began to experience was exacerbated by Savita's fear as well as her excitement. This would be the first time she would travel on the "Grand Vicello" or the "Big Bird" as they translated it. She clung to his arm, her head resting on his shoulder for the entire flight.

Landing in Rome was also a first; they were escorted via carriage to Tivoli. It was here that Davis came to understand the love that Savita harbored for her native customs and land. Miles of serene pastures lay amidst scenic hilltops with herds of sheep dotting the landscape. Children gleefully played as their mothers worked the groves of olive gardens. The beauty of Tivoli cast its majesty upon him. While Savita slept during their rocky trek, Davis combed through the silky strands of her hair, softly massaging her scalp. Unbeknownst to Davis, Savita was awake, lovingly embracing his subtle touch. They arrived in town just before sundown. The narrow streets were lined with onlookers unsure what to make of the sight of this burly, dignified Black man with their Italian belle. Europe had a reputation for social liberalism and acceptance of Blacks, but the small town of Tivoli was an old town, far removed from Italy's urban metropolis like Milan and Naples. Tivoli held true to preserving the local favor, customs and everything Italian, including its women.

Upon arrival, they immediately headed to St. Morize Ospedale where Savita's mother lay gravely ill in the hospital. Her father, Savadore, had abandoned his namesake when she was five years old. On what would soon become her deathbed, her mother, Isabella, lay in the presence of the priest and began to outline her last wishes, leaving to Savita the home in which she was born and raised. Holding her daughter's hand, with a smile and a last gasping breath, Isabella passed away. Savita watched the only person she'd loved pass before her eyes, and again, Davis's presence was there to comfort her. At the moment her mother passed, Savita knew there was no going back to Sigonella. These unfortunate circumstances had brought her back to her first home, Tivoli. This also presented an immediate dilemma for Davis, who had connected with Savita like no one else ever before. Their relationship would be potentially uprooted by Savita's permanent move back to Tivoli.

After the quaint funeral procession and returning to what was now Savita's home; Davis was hesitant to bring up anything in the midst of her mourning, but he could not help yielding to the immediacy of his thoughts. "Savita, sweetheart, how are you? I'm here! I'm not going anywhere," Davis offered. She received this as but a customary offering of condolence, smiling and nodding. The seriousness of Davis's statement had yet to register with her. "No! I mean I'm not going anywhere, I will move here if you desire!" Davis's tone highlighted the clarity of his point. Typical Davis, never shying from unchartered waters, as his spontaneity often held helm. Cupping her cheeks, "Io amare tu!" he said gently, expressing his love, as the corners of her eyes swelled with tears. Savita stood motionless as she commanded his lips in a passionate lock that signaled her approval and reciprocated his love. It was this night thatfell over Tivoli that they made love, satisfying much anticipation and easing much pain. As morning approached and the sun pierced the window, Davis gathered his things to return to the Sigonella Naval base and make his retirement official before returning to marry Savita. With such permanent plans and the implications on his career, he wanted to be assured prior to submitting his resignation. He woke Savita, whose smile preceded the opening of her eyes. Kneeling at the side of her bed, "Marry me!" Davis asked, his question bordering a directive. She abruptly sat up, now fully awake, and tilted her head to clear her hair from her face, pausing to see if she comprehended fully what he'd said. "Yes, si, si, yes!" Savita exclaimed ecstatically, speaking a mixture of Italian and English. She pulled him back into bed for one last erotic send-off.

CHAPTER II

The First Dawn of Tivoli

Their first summer together, 1965, witnessed Tivoli becoming the home of Mr. and Mrs. Davis-Whitmore. They married at the famed Church of San Luigi dei Francesi. Davis had secured a pilot job with the commercial airline, Air Al Italia, as their life was one of modest comfort and convenience. Sadly, their honeymoon was short-lived. Their marriage quickly came under a cloud of public disapproval against culture- and race-mixing. They became subject to rumors; suspicions challenged the core of their marriage. The disapproval was most prevalent in Old-town Tivoli, where the purity of bloodline and cultural preservation was closely scrutinized. Nevertheless, their love was all the Italy they needed.

Italy in 1968 was at the tail-end of a deep recession under President Giuseppe Sarajat. The economic crisis had decimated commercial and industrial centers like Milan, Naples and Venice, and nearly every industry servicing the country. But hit hardest by the downturn were the old Arcadian towns like Tivoli, whose major economic contributor was olive oil production.

The travel industry in particular was hit hard, causing a crunch in the Whitmore household as Air Alitalia cut its flight schedule. Nevertheless the marriage between Davis and Savita remained as strong as the first day he proposed. Their bond had been strengthened by the addition of a beautiful daughter, Mia, whose happy disposition brought a much-needed joy and lessened the family strain. Anyone would have been hard-pressed to find a father/daughter relationship that could parallel the connection and love between Davis and Mia. He affectionately called her "Mia Flower," a name that would carry for years. But his time at home was scant, diminished by his career as a commercial pilot and his second job as a courier for Cavali Oil. This sacrifice would prove to be a turning point for the family. Rumors, precipitated by late nights and envy of local townsmen who were jealous of Davis's status as an outsider, not to mention a Black man, had began to surface. The seeds of sedition began to take root in the Whitmore home, as a once trusting Savita started ranting with unrelenting questions each time Davis would return home. As he began amassing more overtime to bring in extra income, he'd be gone nearly eighteen hours a day. Eventually this was not out of mere financial necessity, but a mode of escape from the stinging pressures at home.

Cavali Oil was a factory housed in an old warehouse where the olive oil was processed and manufactured. Its dark, cold stones added to the drudgery of the desolate environment, where only he and shopkeeper, Vitalia Lucci, worked the evening shift. The business was managed by her Uncle Sonny, but it was Vitalia who owned the business in the absence of her husband, Carmine Lucci. Vitalia's guise as shop and record keeper allowed her to keep a close, unexpected eye on the operation, without gender differences interfering with the work. Vitalia was well-known in her own regard; in her earlier years she had served as the towns' courtier, mastering the art of etiquette, courtesy, seduction, and gamesmanship. Her beauty in the small town was unparalleled. S he was sent away at an early age to study in Venice, but returned to

Tivoli after college. She married the town's most notable and beloved figure, former reputed mob boss, Carmine Lucci. Lucci had been jailed for the car bombing death of a Roman elected official who had targeted Lucci's operation as part of a campaign promise to crackdown on organized crime. Carmine and Vitalia had one daughter, Nadia, who was the same age as the Whitmore's child, Mia.

Turning in his time sheet on a late and stormy fall night, Davis took notice of the young girl's picture on Mrs. Lucci's desk. Davis handed the sheet to her. "Daughter, I assume? She's beautiful! What's her name?" Davis asked, holding the picture in his hand.

"Yes, that's my baby girl. Nadia, she's two," she replied. "She definitely has your eyes." Davis said. His statement was followed by an awkward silence followed, as Vitalia thought Davis must have been checking her out to notice her eyes. "Thank you! Do you have children?" she asked. Reaching to pull out his wallet, beaming with pride, he showed the picture of his daughter Mia. Vitalia attempted to reciprocate the compliment. "Well, she definitely has your…" Vitalia paused, unable to pinpoint a likeness.

"Nothing, she completely favors her mother!" Davis smiled, as they both. Hesitantly and with feigned concern, they noted the time and took leave from one another. Without words, the hint of possibility had been sparked.

Many extended nights followed, accompanied by conversations between the two. Greeting Davis in the darkness of their living room one late evening after work, Savita hurled an accusatory "Davis, where have you been?" in his direction.

"Work, I've been working overtime," a startled Davis answered. "Why are you acting nervous?" After Savita barraged him with an uncharacteristic display of anger, he retorted, "First, you startled me! Second, I'm busting my ass with two jobs to keep food on the table and this is the best you can greet me?" Davis frowned. He shook his head in disgust and slowly walked to the door. Before Savita could get an apology out, the door slammed.

Chapter III

The Forbidden Fruit of Lucci

The recession had taken its toll on the family. Davis felt physically and mentally beaten, and his relationship with Savita suffered most. Now, riding through the town and its barren outskirts, the only signs of life Davis could see beamed from the headlights of a car stopped on the side of the road. Ever the Good Samaritan, Davis stopped to offer assistance. Surprised, he saw, looking up from under the hood, Vitalia. "Hello, Mrs. Lucci. You OK?" Davis asked.

"Never said I knew much about cars, but I think this engine is broke!" Vitalia answered. Davis laughed at her attempt at using mechanical terminology.

"Yes, I believe you're right. Your engine is broke!" he added, both finding laughter in an otherwise distressing moment. Davis was unable to pinpoint the problem with the car, so he offered Vitalia a ride home. She accepted, and Davis opened her door.

"What are you doing out this late?" Vitalia asked.

"Just clearing my head, a ride normally works best for me." Davis replied. They arrived at Vitalia's more than modest villa on the outskirts of Tivoli. Vitalia sensed his frustration and felt a need to offer comfort to Davis.

"Listen, I really appreciate the ride, if you like you can join me for a drink...coffee, whatever." she offered.

"Well, I umm…" Davis failed to complete his thought or sentence. "I guess it's safe to assume that that translates into yes in English!" Vitalia joked, so Davis obliged. He was moved by her confidence and down to earth sense of humor. The night seemed to have slowed amidst their laughter. Their respective aggravations gave way to made grins, and eventually the third glasses of wine began to take their toll, ushering in the vulnerabilities of their senses.

Vitalia, sensing his submissive state, walked around the French provincial lounge where Davis now rested, removing his hat to massage his head. "Vi, Vi wait, wait, you know I'm…," Davis attempted to convey the partially sobering thought of his marital status.

"What? Married, yes, but you're here and that makes you mine!" Vitalia removed her blouse and placed his hands on her exposed breasts, abating any lingering sobriety. He slipped into a state of subconscious erotica, releasing an intoxicated moan. Rising quickly, he grabbed her arms firmly, locking them and gently biting her lips. Reversing her command, he pulled her dress up to expose her wet bareness and gently placed her on top of him. Vitalia saddled and rode him like a prized jockey, until she fell off in a comatose state.

Hours had passed by the time Davis awakened with Vitalia still in his arms. As beautiful as the sun was making its way above horizon, being a dutiful husband he would have much rather been watching its arrival from the confines of his home. "Mrs. Lucci?" Davis began his question.

"No, it's Vitalia!" she corrected him; not wanting to switch back into their business roles yet.

"I'm at a loss for words!" Davis said, a gloss still remaining in his eyes.

"Just tell me you loved it as much as I did?" Vitalia asked, with a look that served as an invitation back. Davis backed towards the door, tipping his hat goodbye, "Si!" he answered, smiling his RSVP.

Driving home seemed to take an eternity. Davis was caught between the feeling of total liberation from the stresses of home and a reasonable excuse he could offer Savita for his absence. But a third and pivotal thought had yet to register. Vitalia was still married to reputed mob boss, Carmine Lucci. Although still incarcerated, he was still beloved and very connected. Returning home, Davis found Savita holding Mia in her arms and looking out the window. There were no visible signs of anger or questions coming forth from Savita. This puzzled Davis, as her silence beckoned an unsolicited explanation more than her words could call to question. "Baby, I'm so sorry I'm late, the…" Davis started to explain. Savita turned to Davis with a subdued half smile. "No need for apologies, no need for explanation." Savita said, sparing herself the insult and further injury from a lie. Davis could not understand the laxity in her response. Then it hit him. He'd totally missed the fact that this was the anniversary of her mother's death.

The late nights and secret escapades continued for twelve summers. Seasons that witnessed Vitalia's daughter Nadia grow to fourteen years of age and Mia to fifteen. They'd developed a friendship of their own, spending every waking moment together in anticipation of the start of high school. Both girls were oblivious to the nature and extent of their parents' relationship but Savita was not. She more than suspected something, but the deep love and admiration that Mia had for her father gave Savita pause when she considered separating the family. She quietly buried her heart in exchange for her daughter's happiness, which was hers as well.

Chapter IV

The Return of Don Carmine

Fifteen years had passed since Carmine Lucci was locked away. Years that bore witness to the forbidden bond growing between Vitalia and Davis. The affair was well hidden by the many late nights of working the factory and the guise of meetings.

The time had come for Tivoli to brace itself for the Don's return. Don Carmine Lucci was a local hero to the Tivolians, a modern-day Robin Hood who had taken from those of ample means, who themselves had taken from the common folk of the towns. His family served as a de-facto government, but one beloved, with more respect and power. He was welcomed by most, yet his return created a dilemma for others, including Vitalia and Davis. The years of hidden suspense and romance had blinded them to this inevitable reality, for which their hearts were ill-prepared. Carmine, although imprisoned in Sardinia, never took his hand off the pulse of Tivoli, especially the activities of his beautiful wife, Vitalia, so it was much to his dismay when he received word of Vitalia's long-running infidelity, and of the American with whom she'd betrayed him.

In the summer of 1983, the streets of Tivoli were filled as if the Pope himself was making an entrance. Cheering crowds of Italians waved the city's crescent emblem and red, white and blue flags, with signs that read "Viva Don Lucci." Savita herself, native to Tivoli, respected and loved Carmine Lucci for his charitable acts and his gentlemanly mannerisms, and his reputation as Tivoli's

"Robin Hood." Remembering that even from prison, Don Lucci had flowers sent to her on the death of her mother. It was a common courtesy Lucci extended to every Tivolian who had passed away, but extraordinary that he would do so even from prison.

Preparing for the parade, she hurriedly readied Mia to catch Carmine's entrance along the route, "Sweetie, are you ready? We're gonna miss it!" Savita asked of Davis, nudging him as he lay motionless on the sofa.

"Can't you see I'm tired, dammit?" Davis retorted, his voice ridden with frustration. Embarrassed, stunned and visibly hurt, Savita flashed a half smile in hopes of disquieting the moment and shield Mia from the pain she felt. Savita and Mia left quietly, without so much as a whisper. Davis's sharp words and unwillingness to accompany her all but confirmed what Savita had long suspected.

Several weeks after Carmine's homecoming, an eternity for Vitalia and Davis, who lay amidst their longest sabbatical apart in nearly fifteen years, Savita bore the emotional residue from this change. It was a Friday afternoon and Davis was settling in to a new assignment in another department at Cavali Oil. Savita, ever the dutiful wife, was at home preparing the evening meal, when three knocks came in rapid succession at the door. It was Don Carmine Lucci, in a rare appearance without his bodyguard. Standing right before her, a man of such legendary and towering stature, a folk legend, hero and the most feared and respected man in Tivoli. "Come sta, Signora Savita Farone," Carmine greeted her in his gentlemanly fashion.

"Sto molto bene Don Lucci." Savita replied that she was well, trying to hide her anxiety at having a reputed mob boss on her doorstep.

"Bene, grazie a tu!" Carmine returned her greeting. "May I come in?" Carmine humbly asked.

"Si, yes, please Don Lucci," Savita said. Don Lucci, who was known for his cool and his humble mannerisms, was also a man of few words. Those he chose to speak were pointed and resolute. "Signora Farone, I must inform you that I strongly suspect your husband has engaged in a long affair with my wife," Lucci said, his tone dropping from humble to somber.

"Don Lucci, God, I'm so sorry. I have no idea!" Savita said offering her apologies for her husband's behavior, fearing what this would mean for her family's safety.

"No need, Madame, to apologize. This is no fault of yours. I only wanted to apprise you, in hopes that you might assist your husband in making wiser choices in the future." Carmine said. As he took his leave of Savita, he smiled, kissed her hand to show his respect and said, "How any man would absence himself from such beauty as yours is a mystery!" He parted with comforting words and compliments to Savita, leaving her feeling worse now, not only from the confirmation of betrayal, but from seeing a gracious, humble man like Don Lucci extend such kindness to the wife of an adulterer. With Lucci's words, an enormous weight was lifted from her aching shoulders. Shutting the door, she knelt, covering her face, and burst into a fray of tears and screams. It wasn't shock, for Don Lucci's visit had been but affirmation. Savita had known of the affair for years, yet her desire to keep her family whole took precedence over any feelings of betrayal. She also knew all too well the danger of taking anything from a man like Don Lucci, and the retaliation that would surely come, yet Davis remained unaware of his wife's knowledge of the affair. Savita was left to balance her emotions with figuring out a rational way to steer the situation into calm, safe waters. Savita settled on engaging in a play to wrestle her husband away from the thrones of his mistress's influence.

She began to encourage her husband to relocate to the United States. Savita's hope was that the distance would discourage the affair and spare the family the drama to which Davis remained oblivious. Months would pass before Davis would acquiesce to her subtle, persistent prodding. Finally, relenting, Davis requested and accepted military reserve re-entry orders to Maxwell Air Force Base in Montgomery, Alabama.

Montgomery was a far cry from the serene hillsides and cobblestone streets of Tivoli. The only memory this southern city conjured up for Davis was that of boycotts and the mistreatment of Blacks during the Civil Rights era of the '50s and '60s. This would be a bittersweet time for the entire Whitmore family. Young Mia had to part with her dearest friend, Nadia. Savita had to say another goodbye to the town she loved more than anything, and Davis was forced to close a chapter in a book he had come to love, a book he still believed no one else was reading, when he said goodbye to Vitalia.

The morning of the family's last moments in Tivoli had arrived. The day none so perfect, with Savita awaking easily as Davis lay on his side, staring out the window. "Good morning, Babe. How you feeling?" she asked gently, sensing the trepidation within him, so certain of the root of his mood she could write its story.

Davis spoke past his pain. "Hey, oh, I'm fine, Honey, just,

umm…looking forward to new challenges!" Davis answered struggling to muster a smile. All of their belongings had been packed and shipped except the remaining luggage which was loaded into the carriage Davis had chartered to take the family to the airstrip. Overcome with the desire to see Vitalia one last time, he needed just a few moments and space to bid his forbidden farewell. "Gee whiz!" Davis exclaimed.

"What, Babe?" Savita asked.

"Oh, I forgot the transfer documents and my passport at the lockbox." Davis said, feigning forgetfulness. "I'll grab a taxi and meet you there. You can't miss our place for boarding." Davis instructed Savita to go ahead as he cheerfully kissed them. Savita figured that all the important documents were really Vitalia, yet she smiled, believing that soon, this saga would be over. Don Carmine Lucci also knew this was the last day that Davis and his family would be in Tivoli, as he kept a watchful eye on Vitalia's movements. Such disrespect, encroaching upon Don Carmine's interest, especially after a courtesy warning, was always dealt with extreme prejudice. Davis, befogged by his passions, was blinded to the risks, though, and he engaged in one last meeting.

...Shadows of a Grave

They planned to rendezvous at an abandoned farmhouse situated about twelve miles outside of Tivoli where he'd occasionally met Vitalia on their getaways. The exterior of the house was dilapidated, but it was finely kept inside. Its outer condition served as a shabby, ruse for unsuspecting guests or trespassers. Reaching the farmhouse in frantic excitement, Davis entered through the back door to an empty, quiet house. Expecting to see Vitalia presenting herself in the seductive, half-naked way she normally greeted him, he noticed instead a paper on the fireplace mantle. It was the copy of his message to Vitalia to meet him. He smiled, calling out to her, knowing that he didn't have much time. "Vitalia, Baby? I give up, come on, Sweetie, we have just a little time!" As Davis's voice echoed through the barren cottage, he realized something was wrong. Vitalia was never late, and especially today, their last day, would've been overwhelmed herself to see him. As he turned to walk out the door, he was startled...by Don Carmine Lucci, his heart's arch nemesis. Davis's knew his fate was sealed here at his destiny's end.

The last words he heard were Don Lucci's..."Why so much disrespect, American? For my town, my woman, for me!" Two gunshots followed before a stunned Davis could offer his plea – one to the chest and one to the head, as he slumped into a pool of blood. Moments later, their once secret love cove burst into a fiery tomb. Lucci set the cottage aflame and watched, holding the crumbled letter tight in his fist, the note that ushered in the demise of their affair and ultimately Davis's life. He finally tossed it into the burgeoning fire, watching it burn to wisps and sparks, before the cottage burst into flames.

29

Chapter V

Lone in the Land of Opportunity

All that time, Mia had waited on the airport tarmac, clutching the chain around her neck, a going-away gift from Nadia. Savita had become anxious as her calls to Davis had gone unanswered. The plane was due to depart in less than thirty minutes for Rome, then head on to its final destination in Alabama. Davis's instructions had always been as military directives that Savita heeded without question; so she and Mia stayed on the plane as he had asked, proceeding in their travel itinerary to Montgomery and Maxwell Air Force base, where they would find Davis's new duty assignment and their new living quarters. Savita had taken comfort in the thought that Davis had always found a way to come through. She had no idea that this time was any different. "Where's Papa?" Mia asked her mother.

"He'll meet us once we get there." Savita said, comforting Mia, whose head rested on her shoulder. Although resolved to stay optimistic, Savita still worried. Hundreds of thoughts traveled her mind, many of suspicion. She pondered the thought of Davis extended last minute tryst with Vitalia, which made her eerily nauseated. Her anger decimated any worry of potential danger. Savita settled with the thought that soon the miles that would separate Davis from Vitalia, if not his willing desire, would bring an end to a dark saga and allow them to start anew. The eight-hour flight from Italy to Alabama landed and they immediately taxied to the Air Base to settle in. Savita contacted the command duty officer to reach the military authorities back in Sigonella to check on

Davis's whereabouts. The duty officer settled them into their temporary quarters and told them he would deliver any information he could find.

The next morning, Savita and Mia awakened to the empty shadows of Davis's absence. Savita took Mia to the mess hall to grab breakfast, trying to push away the anxiety of Mia's growing concern about the whereabouts of her Papa. "Mia, sweetie, your Dad will be here soon. Let's look around. The base doesn't seem too bad, huh?" Savita attempted to ease Mia's concern. After breakfast, they toured the base for a few hours, 'til Savita had had enough, overcome by the anxiety of being in a foreign land absent her husband. She went into the Ombudsman's office, remembering that it was the place tasked with assisting in a wide range of affairs and family issues. "Excuse me sir, I'm Savita Whitmore. I was told to check back with you on word of my husband, Davis Whitmore, back in Tivoli, Italy. He missed our flight."

The uniformed officer rummaged around his desk, finally paging through a file. "Yes ma'am, he was to report for duty at 0900 hours!" he said.

"I know. He was supposed to be on the plane, and I've yet to hear from him," Savita told him, whispering so that Mia wouldn't panic. The officer walked back to his desk, typing into the computer information requesting updates on the military's wire system that accounted for current developments of AWOLs, last minute reassignments, and emergencies. "Excuse me ma'am. I'll be right back." The officer turned and hurried into his superior's office. At this point, Savita felt the queasiness of a stomach virus and distressing doubts began crowding the optimism out of her thoughts. She idled nearer to the inner office, trying to get a peek of what was going on. By now, four officers had joined the desk clerk in Staff Sergeant Slate's office, the Command Duty Officer. One officer wore a Cross insignia on his lapel and had armed himself with a Bible.

Staff Sgt. Slate leaned back into his chair after hanging up from the call. "Mrs. Whitmore…" The Chaplain who wore the cross insignia began.

"Wait, Mia, dear, can you wait here for a moment?" Savita asked Mia, sensing it was troubling news.

"Ma'am, I'm deeply sorry to inform you…" Staff Sgt. Slate began.

"No, please, tell me no!" Savita said with a long, soft and weary voice, trying her best to compose herself for Mia, whom she knew would be devastated beyond coping.

"Your husband was reported missing. Remains have been found and identified as his…Ma'am, I'm truly sorry." he said, completing his formal condolences. This time, though, Staff Sgt. Slate was particularly moved. He and Davis had served a tour together in Sigonella back in 1959. It was through his connection to Staff Sgt. Slate that Davis had been able to secure his expedited orders to Maxwell Air Force Base, highly desirable relocation orders. Savita didn't know how to tell her daughter. She had never imagined having to do so. The Chaplain grabbed Savita's hand, walking together with her to break the news to Mia. Staff Sgt. Slate jumped in front of the two as if he were taking a bullet on the battle field for a comrade. "Mia, I've known your Dad for over twenty-five years. We were together when he first came to Italy….dear, I'm so sorry to tell you that your father is…hummh, umh, he's deceased." Slate said struggling to look into the eyes of this young girl who adored and idolized her father. Mia looked puzzled, and as the realization hit her, Savita grabbed her and tucked her head into her bosom, the tears causing her shirt to stick to her skin.

Suddenly, instead of a fresh new start, Savita and Mia faced a foreign land, where the South was foreign within its own nation's borders; stranded without the strength, security and guidance of their lifelong soldier. In one short conversation, their world was irreparably shattered.

Savita knew, though, that she had to move forward, to not miss a beat, and by doing so perhaps salvage at least a degree of the security she lost with her husband. There would be no burial ceremony, because there was no body to salute; only the memory and a military portrait of a young Davis, and a folded American flag given to Mia on behalf of her father.

The Military Unit provided whatever the family needed to transition. They provided a stipend and the small insurance policy that had come with his military benefit package. They offered housing accommodations, but Savita chose to turn instead to the one place in America she was familiar with, the place she had family ties…. Saint Louis, Missouri.

CHAPTER VI

St. Louis Blues

Moving to St. Louis involved culture shock, but not as much as would have greeted them in Montgomery. Family on both sides lived in St. Louis. Savita's Italian relatives lived in the quaint Southwest section of the city known as "The Hill," or "Little Italy," and the Black relatives on Mia's father's side resided on the city's predominately Black North side.

Savita, still in shock from the death of her husband and with no ties of kinship, knew that finding living accommodations for her and Mia would be a titanic challenge. She turned to a great-uncle, Uncle Armando. Uncle Armando had migrated from Sardinia during the second exodus of the immigrant wave from Western Europe in the late 1920s.

He found them a tidy brick bungalow with a neatly manicured lawn, situated in a well-kept, self-sustaining neighborhood. Savita and Mia found every Italian social fancy provided by its locals - Italian eateries, bakeries, grocers, bars, and cleaners. At first glance, this seemed to make for an easy social transition for Mia and her mother. It was an urban model of small town Tivoli. But Savita encountered the same ire of a very traditional Italian uncle, as when she first took up with Davis in Sigonella. They shunned the very thought of such a beautiful Italian woman mixing with a black man, which left Mia, her face belying the black blood mixed into her Italian heritage, an outsider everywhere. She was shunned in school and on playgrounds not only amongst Italians, but other whites who

34

embraced an even more scornful resentment of blacks and of race-mixing. As beautiful as Mia was, she quickly became a social pariah amongst her peers. After an attack by a group of young girls on the schoolyard grounds left her daughter covered with scrapes and bruises, Savita had had enough. She lifted herself out of the abyss of numbing pain, climbing up and over the cultural challenges and the loss of Davis, and for Mia, mustered the courage to move to the North side of town, in hopes of engaging Davis's aunt's support. His aunt owned a four-family flat on a quiet street next door to Cupples Elementary School. Savita had never met any of Davis's family. Reaching out was nothing less than a cold call. Given few other options, Savita phoned Davis's Aunt Loretta. She hesitantly dialed the numbers on the phone, as it rang. "Yes?" the woman picked up.

"Yes ma'am, ummh, my name is Savita, Savita Farone-Whitmore…"

Savita began her introduction, but the woman interrupted, "Yes, baby, Davis's wife. How are you and that lovely grandniece of mine doin'?" Aunt Loretta asked. Savita was taken aback by Loretta's warmth and familiarity; her manner was a comforting contrast to the Italian family reactions in South Saint Louis.

"We're as well as can be expected," Savita said. "We've settled in St. Louis, and Davis always said that if there was ever anyone one can turn to, it would be you," she added.

"Bless his soul. He was always one of my favorites." Savita could hear the smile in her voice.

"Ma'am, we really need a place to stay until we get on our feet,"

Savita asked.

"Say no more, you just bring your things right over." Aunt Loretta had an available unit in the four-family flat, and she opened it to Savita and Mia for as long as they needed. Ironically, their temporary residence had been the Carousel Motel, just a few blocks away and a well-known, unsavory haven for drug traffic and prostitutes. Savita had sensed the environment was of suspect character, but not to the depths in which she was fortunate to now be spared. As the two stepped out of the cab with their luggage in tow, Aunt Loretta, a tall, dark-skinned, silver-haired lady, whose strength was evidenced by the veins protruding from her gangly arms, greeted them. "So this is Mia Flower?" Auntie said, drawing a smile from Mia with the pet name her father called her. "And dear Savita, you're even more beautiful that Davis described!" Loretta exclaimed, hugging them as tears rolled from their eyes. It all reminded Savita of Davis and the newness of his absence. Mia had been mute throughout their conversations, until Aunt Loretta brought out the photo albums. She gave Mia a pictorial tour of her father's life. "And here's a picture of him holding you when you were born," flipping the page. "This is one of your mother and father, on their first date outside the theatre." Mia was fully engaged, peppering Loretta with questions of her Dad. Savita smiled, quietly reminiscing, amazed that Davis had safeguarded their pictures and shared them with his family. All of their struggles and challenges were suddenly supplanted by the goodness of the memories, of his soft charm and the considerate qualities that endeared him to her and immortalized Davis in the eyes of Mia.

Afterward, they settled into their shotgun apartment, which was already partially furnished. Savita knew she had to gently usher Mia into her new environment. She began by enrolling her into Charles

Sumner High School in the Historic Ville neighborhood. The irony that such great loss had brought Mia to this school was not lost on Savita. She knew that world-renowned opera singer, Grace Bumbry, had attended Sumner High, and both Davis and Savita had enjoyed the likes of her performances. The school was also a Midwestern Mecca for high school football. Unfortunately, it also bore a growing reputation for skirmishes, especially amongst squabbling teenage girls. This was a phenomenon foreign to the more sedate school grounds of a place like Tivoli, where the most notable indiscretions included putting gum in someone's seat and clique exclusions from school yard activities.

Mia's first day of school was utterly forgettable, one of the loneliest since the plane ride without her father. Walking into her home class, Mia drew sharp stares and pointed sneers from the students. Maybe it was her conservative, homely attire; but more likely the girls found Mia's beauty both intimidating and inviting to the males they courted. She was shunned, almost going without lunch to avoid the dining hall. Mia finally faced the lunch crowd, whose seats were always accounted for by the many cliques. Mia approached another table where three girls sat, expecting the customary "*this seat is taken*," and hovered slowly nearby. Instead, one of the girls glanced up at her. "What? You're going to eat standing? Girl, sit down!" she said, extending the rare courtesy of high school lunch room hospitality.

"Thank you!" Mia said, relief giving way to a smile.

"I'm Pam, this is Melanie and Sheree." Pam said introducing the table as Mia breathed a sigh of relief and quickly sat down.

Pam was a junior and one of the most popular girls in school. She was a fast-talking, hip girl, whose reputation seemed to be that of the easy girl. This, at least for the high school boys, was a positive draw. But Pam was more notably the daughter of "Big Red" Wright, one of the most powerful and respected street bosses in St. Louis. Although Mia's naiveté, fashion-challenged attire and freshmen class status would have normally relegated her to the lower rungs of the school's social order, Pam nevertheless embraced Mia, instantly giving Mia cool points and credibility with the in-crowd. With the ever-cunning Pam, this was probably more about icing her potential competition, but for Mia, life at school was no longer the hell of the Southside. Pam knew that the young men who normally clamored for her would definitely salivate at a fine, fresh new face like Mia's. Throughout the next few semesters, Mia and Pam's relationship outpaced and outgrew the others, as both were introduced and welcomed by their respective families. Inwardly, Mia's mother, worried about Pam's influence on Mia. Big Red welcomed Mia as a positive addition, and knowing that she'd lost her beloved father, even offering her his own paternal covering by "adopting" her as his god-daughter.

Mia slowly shed her social inhibitions and began relaxing her conservative dress for more fashionable digs, soon attracting the interest of the basketball team's star forward, Lawrence "The Meal Ticket" Michael. Lawrence was aptly named "The Meal Ticket" for his prowess on the basketball court and his potential landing a lucrative professional contract. Although Michael was one of the most popular and well-liked student athletes, he was reserved, modest and detached from most extracurricular activities of youthful indiscretion. They were like-natured teenagers whose personality traits made them a natural fit. Pam, who had never approached Lawrence, was always secretly attracted to him, but knew her reputation alone figured her incompatible. Yet, she was happy for Mia, who had become a social butterfly and popular amongst a cross section of jocks, nerds, stoners and loners.

Mia was crowned Homecoming Queen her junior year, alongside Lawrence as King. Tensions increased between them during their senior year, when Lawrence accepted a scholarship offer from UCLA, halfway across the country. Mia, now 18, was crushed to later find out that Lawrence had been secretly seeing a college girl from UCLA whom he met on a college recruiting visit. The betrayal tore at Mia. Up to this point, she had only two men in her life…her father and Lawrence. She turned to Pam, who, over the past four years, had become her closest friend, for comfort.

Pam had graduated a year earlier, had her own place and had quickly jumped into a social frenzy of non-stop partying and getting high. Lawrence and Mia broke up on prom night. Mia called Pam, who was heading out to Club 618 across the river in East St. Louis. She invited Mia along. "What's up, girl? Look, don't sweat it. Let's roll to the club…it's a hundred Lawrences there!" Pam coaxed Mia out of the pre-stages of an emotional slump.

"I dunno. Girl you know it's 24 and up. I can't swing that!" Mia whined.

"Girl, I gotchu! I know the manager well," Pam countered.

"Ah-ite girl, come swoop me." Mia finally caved in.

The After Set

Entering the club, Mia had to adjust to a new vibe, a departure from her high school set. All the people, of course, were much older, yet her ability to turn heads proved undiminished. Pam immediately took her into the VIP area where Brandon "Bri" Baptiste and his guest parlayed. "Heyyy, Bri!" Pam said as she approached the table.

"What's up Lil Red, you stayin' out of trouble?" Bri asked, affectionately using the name 'Lil Red' with respect to Pam's father, Big Red, whom he'd groomed in the intricacies of the hustler life from the beginning of his teen years. Mia stood by silently, trying her best not to display immaturity and exposure her age. She waited until Pam made the introduction. "Oh, this is my homegirl Mia," she said.

Bri smiled with slow repetitious nods, "Well, hello young lady. Anything you need…it's on me, enjoy yourself." he said, with a coolness that masked his intent of seduction.

"Thank you," Mia replied as the two held a momentary glance before she turned away and he resumed the conversation of his company. Mia remained reserved most of the night, sitting back and casually observing Pam spread her social wings, enjoying a bird's eye view of the dance floor.

Bri, meanwhile, inconspicuously locked her in on his player's scope from afar. "Beauty begets beauty," Bri always thought, as he rationalized Mia as a potential tender arm piece who could draw others. As the night drew to a close and the last call went out from the DJ booth, Bri offered Mia a ride home because Pam was visibly in no condition to drive. He relished the opportunity to acquaint himself with Mia alone, so he let Pam stay in the residential loft atop the club, much better than clouding the mood with an intoxicated, back seat distraction.

Mia cautiously accepted the long ride home from East St. Louis to Kingshighway and Cote-Brilliante in his 1989 Jaguar XJS with a subdued excitement. She was careful not to say anything that might underscore the age and maturity gap between the two. Bri, calculating, let the music relax her and pave the entry into her psyche, more than his words could possibly do. He set his music to the extended versions of the Moment's *"Sexy Mama"* and *"For You,"* two soulfully smooth, deeply sensual basement funk tracks that massaged the mind and primed the appetite for intimacy. Cautious to not overreach, he held back as he pulled up at her flat. "Well young lady, here you are. I hope you enjoyed yourself, I know the seat did!" Bri joked referring to all the time Mia spent sitting down.

"Well, Mr. Bri…," she began.

"No, just Bri, please!" he interrupted, extending her the informality of address.

"Well, Bri, thank you and yes, my seat and I enjoyed ourselves," she smiled as she exited the Jag.

"Wait a minute, if you're not doing anything next week, why don't you join me. Mikki Howard is my guest and you can join us in VIP," Bri offered.

Mia tried not to appear too eager. "Let me check my schedule and I'll get back at you," she said.

Bri knew it was a ploy, but respected her attempt at the semblance of game. "OK, young lady, you have a restful night." Bri drove off, leaving Mia wishing she had eyes in the back of her head to capture Bri's gaze from the rear. Somewhere between the first hello, the drive home and the music, intrigue lit a mutual spark that beckoned them to learn of one another.

The ride home from the club and the flirtatious overtures by Bri were enough to send young Mia reeling. Successful, popular and charming, Bri had cut through all the layers of post-pubescent emotional defenses that Mia might hold against the much older man, and he knew it. Lying on the couch, unable to sleep, Mia called Pam to check to see if she was OK. "Hey girl, you cool?" Mia asked a slurred-speech Pam.

Clearing her throat, "Yeahhh, ummh, I'm ah-ite," Pam said sighing a tired breath.

Insistent on having a conversation, in spite of Pam's altered state, "Wazzup witcha boy?" Mia asked with a giddy uncharacteristic slang.

Pam wiped the sleep from her eyes. "Whatchu talking about, girl?" Pam asked. "Bri?"

Mia answered. "He drove me home."

"You little hussy! He tasted that crème brulée, didn't he?" Pam teased.

"Nope, that's your steelo, easy breezy!" The previously ghetto-challenged Mia shot back as if she'd been injected with 10 ccs of linguistic cool from the needle of Bri's presence.

"Girl he cool, you gotta just get to know him….take your time!"
Pam offered. "Ah-ite girl, my momma coming, gotta go!" Mia
hurried off the phone as she heard her mother's car door shut. She
feigned sleep when mother walked through the door and into Mia's
room. Mrs. Whitmore stared tenderly at her beautiful daughter,
thinking how much her baby girl had grown up, and wishing that
Davis were here to see it.

CHAPTER VII

Chocolate City

Over the few months following her graduation, Bri spent a lot of time and resources trying to cement himself in Mia's psyche. She was a constant at his club, receiving VIP treatment and eventually assuming a matriarchal status. Bri, never outwardly bold in his tactical approaches, chose subtle expressions of his affection. The flowers and gifts without occasion, spur-of-the-moment privately catered lunches, and midday 'just–because' phone messages. But, the summer had nearly passed and the fairy tale that began the night she first met Bri seemed to be nearing its end. Mia had been wrangling with her mom about not going away to collcge, unable to admit to herself, let alone to her mother, that the real reason she was reluctant to part from St. Louis was…Bri! Savita would hear nothing of Mia not going away. She reminded Mia of her commitment to her father to complete her college education. Mia had been accepted to Hampton University in Virginia, and Howard University in Washington, D.C. She reluctantly made the bittersweet decision to move to D.C. and attend Howard; temporarily shattering her desire to secure her own Prince Charming that she romanticized in Bri. Financially, money had been tight for Savita. Mia's scholarship covered full tuition, but only partial room and board, and the east coast housing market ranked costly. Upon finding out about Mia's fall departure and her family's financial predicament, Bri had pre-paid the uncovered housing expenses without their knowledge. With all of the psychological, mental and financial resources that Bri expended on wrapping her up, he had yet to key the locks of her intimate being and cast his web inside her. It would be the final leg of his race to fortify himself within her emotional psyche.

If the transition from Italy to St. Louis had been challenging, her move to D.C. from St. Louis was more of a catastrophic culture shock. The East Coast was faster-paced, especially D.C., a cosmopolitan mix of every social, racial and economic walk of life. The nation's capital was also a city of power, home to political intrigue and scandal. Its flair tended to age one in maturity, and expose those previously lacking worldly perspective to the gift of game that generated hustle and appetites of money and power. But Mia remained tempered by the humility instilled by her parents, especially her father, who shunned the egotistical nature of titles and the trappings that the chase for such things commonly brought. Or maybe she was subconsciously tempered by the trappings of Bri's web of charming deceit and blinding false pleasures, things of which she wasn't yet aware. In time, Mia acclimated to the college experience. Whether by a commitment to which she unknowingly obligated herself or thought of pursuing something with Bri, she restricted herself from dating. Because Mia had been accepted into one of the university's most sought-after classes, Urban Government taught by Professor J.R. Henry, immersing herself in study was easy. Professor Henry was one of the school's most exciting, popular and thought-provoking scholars.

He was popular throughout the east coast and well-known amongst the area's noted academicians and Black intelligentsia. He was a former Black Panther, community activist and a fiery orator who was believed and accepted by the common masses of D.C. as a leader, and whose support was sought by many. Many well-known community leaders, stakeholders, elected officials and civic leaders were guest speakers as part of Professor Henry's lecture series.

There would be one that would leave an indelible mark on Mia, who had become one of the Professor's most engaging students. Walking in class, Mia's aura, of both beauty and intelligence, commanded everyone's attention. "Hello, Professor Henry! Who's speaking today?" Mia asked. The professor usually posted each speaker's name, but would occasionally add to the intrigue by not announcing the guest.

At that very moment, walking boldly onto the stage toward the podium was popular D.C. Mayor, Marion McNarry. Mia was moved by the forty-five minute speech the mayor delivered, more than any previous lecture. No one before had motivated her to expand her interests into the public affairs and government arena. After the lecture ended, Mayor McNarry inquired about the young woman in the front row, asking to be introduced to Mia. "Mia, come please, I want to introduce you." Professor Henry motioned to Mia. "Mr. Mayor this is, by far, one of my favorite students; she may one day challenge you for your seat!" Professor said, jokingly introducing Mia to the mayor.

"Well, when I see her coming I'd best just retire!" Mayor McNarry responded.

"Hello Mayor. I thoroughly enjoyed your lecture." Mia said in humble admiration.

"You can't be from D.C., because I would have heard about such beauty by now from the Capitol to City Hall!" The mayor's well-known charm, illuminated by his power, which had captivated so many lovely young ladies before, was turned up for Mia's benefit.

Honored, Mia could only muster a barely-audible "Thank you, Mr.

47

Mayor!"

Mayor McNarry handed her his card before parting company. "If I can help in any way, please...please, call me," he said, and with a slight nod, grabbed and held her hand, as he bid her farewell.

"That's quite impressive, Mia!" Professor Henry said, noting the attention his own mentor had paid his top student.

"Wow! That was incredible!" Mia's youthful exuberance sparkled.

"Just make sure to follow up with him. His office would serve you well for a summer internship," the Professor added.

Weeks after the initial meeting, Mia called the mayor with the hope of securing a summer internship or work within the government sector. Mia mustered the courage to make the call by doing so in the presence of the professor. As she wiggled her fingers to loosen the rigidity that nearly prevented her from dialing, the professor watched, moved by Mia's innocence and excitement, and wishing he was twenty-five years younger. He shot her his best mentor's smile, keeping her oblivious to the full scope of his thought.

A split-second of numbness overcame her when the mayor himself answered the phone. "Hello, this is Marion McNarry."

"Yes, um, Mr. Mayor, this is Mia Farone, from..."

The mayor cut her off. "Please, Mia how could I forget? And please, call me Marion. How can I help you?" he asked.

"Well, I have the summer open and I'm looking for opportunities to do an internship," Mia said.

"I'd be honored to have you work in my office. Come see me next week and we'll work out the details." he said, sensing her enthusiasm. The mayor was moved by her level of excitement, but more by her youth, beauty and intellect. He looked forward to her presence in his office.

Nine months had passed since Mia had seen Bri. Although they'd developed a cozy friendship over the phone, Mia was kept busy by her on-campus activities. She'd developed a longing crush on the much older Bri in his absence and was excited to call home to tell of her encounter with the mayor.

She called her mother first, whose excitement was tempered and measured. "Momma, you'll never guess who I'm interning for!" Mia gushed.

"I give up!" Savita said, bypassing a guessing game. "The mayor, Ma, Mayor McNarry!" Mia answered.

Because she knew that Mia still bore the innocence of an impressionable young girl who longed for the endearing qualities of a father figure, Savita was always concerned about her daughter's ability to navigate the social circles of men, especially of an esteemed caliber. She hesitated, then forced a smile into her voice. "That's wonderful, my Mia. Just stay focused and mind your lady," Savita told her, referencing the old Italian adage about upholding your womanly manners.

"I will, Ma, I promise!" she said, grateful for her mother's approval. Bri, on the other hand, would not be so receptive to her good news.

Turning her attention to Bri, who she hadn't seen in months, Mia's excitement spilled over the phone line to him. The phone rang, "Well hello, stranger!" Bri answered the line. "Now I'm convinced I'm a blessed man!" Bri said, moved by her call.

"What you been up to, stranger yourself?" Mia asked.

"Just been sitting on my couch waiting for you to call," Bri joked, drawing a smile from the other end of the line.

"What eva! You smoove, but ain't dat smoove for me to believe dat!" Mia countered his flattery, and was amused by his humor. They continued volleying cordial and insignificant conversation.

"So what you got planned for your summer break?" Bri asked.

"Working in Mayor McNarry's office! He's so great, and he chose me for an internship!" Her excitement was palpable. Bri held the phone momentarily, feeling an immediate sense of competing interest over the influence of Mia.

Bri knew he couldn't begin the game by appearing overly interested and jealous, so he chose subtlety and encouraged this working agreement between the two, all the while casting his unsuspecting line into the naïve river of her youth. "Now, I know ain't nobody castin' their lot with my girl?" Bri asked, with just enough jest to keep it light.

"Nawwh, it ain't even like that…he's not even my type!" Mia said, finding herself explaining.

"Gotta her!" Bri thought. Although there was no formal commitment between them and thus no explanation warranted, she caught herself wondering why she felt the need to explain. "Well, what's your type then, Mia Farone?" Bri asked, taking her further off guard.

Stilled in momentary silence…. "That's a very good question, Mr. Brandon. I'll explore that and get back to you." Mia said, mustering the best response she could.

"So you stayin' through the summer all by your lonesome in D.C.?" Bri asked, switching conversational gears.

"Yeah, what's my alternative?" She volleyed his veiled question.

"Welllll, Ms. Mia Farone, I would incline myself to visit, if your schedule and desire would so avail itself." Bri offered the privilege of his presence for a brief summer stay to close the discomfort of her potential loneliness.

"I guess I'll just have to reconcile my desire with my schedule and open it up for such an offer," Mia told him.

"Good! I'll be on a plane in twenty-four hours!" Bri said, once again taking her off guard. Mia was moved by his response. Maybe his interest had finally moved beyond the cat and mouse theatrics of small talk to a more serious stage of intimate engagement.

"I will see you then!" she said, "Gotta go!"

"All right, young lady, have a restful night." Bri hung up the phone.

Mia lay back, in a state of youthful bliss, her head full of the potential of what was to come.

BRI TAKES D.C.

'Just twenty-four hours from womanhood," Mia thought; ready to give herself to a man she had already touched in her mind, in so many ways. She felt like she was standing on the front of a tightly coiled spring before even a kiss had taken place.

Bri, being true to his word, caught the first flight out to D.C. Mia began mentally preparing herself for his arrival, tempering her enthusiasm and expectations to lessen potential disappointment. She had an off-campus apartment, thanks to Bri's secret benevolence. Mia rushed to the corner Dollar Store to pick up some things to spruce up the décor and bought some tapes she knew would appeal to Bri's musical interest - Marvin Gaye, Isley Brothers, Maze, etc.. She hoped this might bridge the obvious age gap between them. For hours, Mia fought the anxiety of giving herself for the first time, not knowing the how's, where's and when' s of intimacy. She'd even rented some adult films, hoping for a quick tutorial for what she wanted to be the inevitable.

Meanwhile, Bri relaxed, sipping wine just twenty minutes away from landing at D.C.'s Dulles International Airport. He made reservations at one of D.C.'s most luxurious hotels, the Hay-Adams, which was as infamous and internationally known as the White House itself. He didn't inform Mia of his presence right away, letting her wonder if perhaps it had been just flirtatious talk after all. Mia had not heard from him all day; she had no idea whether he planned to follow through with his visit or not. Alone and unable to reach him, she felt disappointed and a little foolish. She undressed, putting on a robe and switching on "Lady Sings the Blues." Campus life was bustling with activity on the weekend so on-campus and near off-campus housing was emptied, leaving Mia feeling more lonely than usual. She broke her word to herself to not call Bri and rang his phone. "Hey, what's up?" Mia said trying hard to mask her disappointment as Bri picked up her call.

"Nothing much, how are you?" Bri said calmly with no mention of not coming.

"Humh!" Mia thought, still trying to refrain from coming off too anxious. Unable to hold any longer… "I thought I would probably see you this weekend, but I knew D.C. was probably too big for you!" Mia teased, challenging his ego. Unbeknownst to her, Bri sat right outside her door all the while.

"Yeah, maybe you right!" Bri said, as there was a knock on the door. "Hold on one sec Bri," she said.

"Hold on! What, you got a date or somethin'?" he asked.

"Well, I thought I did!" she said, lightly scolding him. "Ah-ite, hold on player!" Mia said again, placing Bri on hold as she answered the door. There he stood, with a bouquet-mix of Stargazer lilies and African violets and a bottle of wine. She was speechless, flattered by and completely smitten with his surprise presence. Suddenly embarrassed, she turned to run and put back on the clothes she'd just shed.

"No, you are perfect! No need for that!" Bri said. That precious moment of awkwardness arrived, the crossroads of anticipation and the first intimate touch. Mia was frozen at that intersection… but Bri commandeered the moment, grabbing her waist, pulling her close and kissing her on the cheek. He moved far enough to break the ice, just thawing the chill enough to spread warmth through her body without rushing her past a state of calm and comfort. He understood that no matter how cool she tried to play it, she was young.

Her pheromones hinted of the newness of an untapped well, the freshness of a ripe olive ready for picking. This thrilled Bri more than she knew, but he remained firmly in control. In this moment, he was confident he would cast his die inside her, - in her mind, in her heart. "Hey, as much as I hate to ask you to do so…why don't you put your clothes on and let's step out?" Bri asked, even as he took delight in seeing Mia's curvaceous body in her loungewear.

"Okaaay," she said in a girlishly submissive tone. Bri was more a gentleman than Mia had ever known, opening doors, extending delicious compliments, and now showing her a world of class and stately indulgences as they arrived by cab at the Hay-Adams in Lafayette Square.

The Well of Womanhood

The legendary, Italian Renaissance-styled hotel was filled with notoriety and was one of D.C.'s most revered landmarks. Leading authors, writers, politicians, the likes of Mark Twain and famed sculptor, August Saint-Gaudens, had all graced the 16th Street wonder. Bri led Mia toward the five-star Lafayette Room, a renowned culinary Mecca. "Right this way, Mrs. and Mr. Baptiste!" the concierge greeted them. Mia smiled as Bri failed to correct the wait staff, leaving the thought of them as a couple hanging in the air.

The imported Italian marble floor was polished to shine so high it reflected the exquisite French chandeliers suspended from the vaulted ceilings and walnut wainscoting with Tudor and Italian motifs. Original paintings by Modigliani, Picasso, and Rembrandt adorned the walls. Before they'd even placed their orders, Mia's taste was filled by the ambiance and her thirst satiated by Bri's mere presence. Mia's awe was heightened by an unparalleled view of the White House that made dinner all the more appetizing.

"May I offer the suggestions of our night's specials?" The server asked. "Thank you, but we're ready. She'll have the pistachio encrusted Virginia lamb loin with creamy white polenta, and I'll take the eggplant and Vermont chevre cannelloni gratin with red pepper and San Marzano tomato sauce." Bri asserted command as he ordered for them both. "Oh, sir, and please bring a bottle of your vintage Tuscan red." Bri added.

As the pianist played in the background, Mia felt like her womanhood matured from girl to woman in less than an hour. She was holding her own, but was nearing the point of waywardness amidst the forest of Bri's seduction. They filled the next hour with small talk of happenings of St. Louis and campus life in D.C., as the Tuscan red began to take its toll on Mia. Her eyes beamed with the glow of want, as her body slackened like prey in the grasp of an eagle's talons. "Would you like to accompany me to my suite, you seem tired, and there's definitely enough room," Bri asked gently.

"Wellll, I umh…." Mia felt almost incoherent.

"I won't bite, I promise!" Bri smiled. Taking her by the hand, he escorted her to the glass elevator and they traveled slowly, eighteen floors to his suite.

Bri's suite was an immaculate display of stately accommodation that surpassed even the folklore of the Hay-Adams as Mia imagined. She went to the window overlooking Washington's most notable monuments and attractions. Bri slowly walked behind Mia, brushing his hand through her silken hair, removing her blazer. Looking seductively into her eyes, the glossy-mist of which signaled a completely subdued Mia, he whispered, "Thank you. I'm gonna tell you something that I don't commonly say. You are the most beautiful lady I've seen and desired in as long as my memory can recall!" Bri said.

As if the wine hadn't intoxicated her enough, his words threw her into a drunken state of sensuous longing. She felt wetness and a tingle amidst the inner reaches of her thigh that she had never experienced. "Thank you, I really enjoyed your company too, Bri," Mia said, as Bri planted a kiss, alternating between her soft, olive-toned cheeks, her forehead, and the corners of her lips. One long stare locked their gazes and lips, as his tongue finally made entry, waltzing into mouth, satisfying her palate. They slowly danced to the words of Marvin Gaye's *"Come Live With Me Angel,"* while her mind-synced a chorus of Betty Wright's *"Tonight is the Night."* Bri led her from the window, backing her up gently toward the king-sized bed, coaxing her down with their lips still engaged, until he finally laid her down. As he stood over her, Mia lay with one arm outstretched, the other draped across her breast as her eyes and body beckoned Bri for instruction. He unbuttoned his shirt, removing it to expose a chiseled physique and Chinese calligraphy tattooed across his chest. His abdominal muscles rippled, cascading toward his manscape. Mia's heart raced as she wondered what lay beyond the Calvin Klein waistband. Bri braced himself parallel atop of her body. "Relaaax, I got you baby! This is what you been waiting and wanting, huh?" he whispered seductively, simultaneously drawing the tip of his tongue around the outer and inner tracks of her ears. "You want me?" he asked.

"Yeeeesss!" Mia said. Bri slowly rolled her blouse over her head, exposing perky nipples that stood at attention, causing his mouth to water. He began circling round her nipples, holding her breast with a kiss as his tongue rotated with perfect pressure and light graze of teeth that drew moisture from her inner walls like a well.

She was primed for entry, but not before Bri traveled his tongue from her breast to her navel, working her pants down over her hips. When Mia tried to assist him, "No, just lay, relax and wait for me, I got this!" Bri said, dropping the pants onto the floor. He abruptly interrupted the course of his southern oral travel, going north from her perfectly manicured feet, placing every toe in his mouth, driving his tongue separately around each, offering his lips as compression firmly against the middle core of her feet.

Mia began to pant, "Hummm, ummh, humh!" as Bri worked his mouth slowly up the inner side of her left leg as his hand and nails traveled slowly up the right, until he arrived. Bri lifted up, biting his lip and catching her eye as he dipped his index finger inside her. She watched him lick his finger after each thrust. His finger pried the walls of her love well open, but not enough for entry, so he spread her lips wider, exposing her clit, hardening his tongue to its hardest capability, pressing firm upon and fast around it. Using a whirlwind of breathe, he created suction enough to fill her nerve endings with blood, taking her to the brink while his finger continued to thrust inside her. Mia's moans became more pronounced, as she used words not of her normal vocabulary, "Oh, please? Make love to me!" she pleaded.

Bri stood up and slowly lowered his pants, confirming the Haitian folklore of well-endowed men. Mia gasped, wondering how she could possibly welcome all of him inside her. "Bri, wait, wait, I, I...I can't take it!" Mia mumbled, her tone ridden with a mixture of extreme pleasure and intense pain.

"Are you my soldier, baby? Take it for daddy!" Bri instructed, and Mia did so dutifully. Mia longed for Bri inside her, yet nervousness shown clear in her eyes and her body began to shake nervously. Bri raised her legs, spreading them to their upward expanse, struggling to guide himself as carefully and painlessly as possible inside of her. He tried to lessen her pain by distracting her with passionate kissing, leaving his tongue combing her mouth to prevent her from screaming. Although it increased the moist flow of her juices, she still panted and tensed her body with every slow thrust, until finally Bri sat completely inside, filling every centimeter of her inner walls, seemingly stretching it to its expanse. Mia grabbed Bri's back, leaving gashes on him like the back of beaten slave. Her body began to experience a physical phenomena she'd never felt before, as her abdomen began to tense, mouth became parched, one leg rigid and shaken. Her body began to convulse as she lodged her nails deeper into his back. Bri sensed the imminence of her orgasm and grabbed her hair almost violently, pulling it back, his fingers firmly gripped against her scalp, confounding and intensifying every open point of pleasure. Rapidly increasing the speed and depth of his thrusts, "Is this all for me? Say it!" Bri commanded.

"It's yours, it's all yours, baby!" Mia responded, letting out a scream that Bri was sure would draw the attention of the hotel's other guests. Mia reached her climax, placing her hands on his chest as to signal him not to move, as she became overly sensitive to any continued stimulation. Mia rolled over, spread-eagle, as if she was making snow angels on the sheets. She finally cuddled with the pillow between her legs, as the last trails of sweat from the intense round of sexual jousting saturated the sheets. The humidity from the sexually intense friction, completely layered her wrap- hairdo and the Chinese bangs that she had just styled hours before. She cupped herself, attempting to stop her wet bareness from palpitating. Bri watched her, smiling from the lounge chair adjacent the bed; his sexual-ego bolstered as he watched post-orgasmic bliss sedate Mia, the pleasure audible in her sighs until she finally fell into a coma-like sleep. He knew, as the light of that first morning encroached upon the dark recesses of night, that their lives would be impacted - but never could he have imagined or even cared, then, how great its impact would be. For Bri, women were about conquest, feeding his ocean-sized ego. But there was something about Mia that upgraded her pawn-like status on his life's board of chess. Standing on the balcony, waiting to greet the morning like a prize-fighter waits for the opening bell in the ring, Bri talked on the phone while taking in the scenic view of the early sun, peeking over the Potomac River. Mia finally awoke, her smile wide, belying the internal bliss of crossing the threshold of womanhood. In just one night, Mia had matured by years. Bri had to make way quickly to the airport to return to St. Louis. Mia could not avert her stare quick enough before Bri caught her glance fixated on him on the balcony. Bri turned to flash a smile, blowing a kiss to punctuate the lingering thought that he wagered she was thinking. "What's up, Babe? How you sleep?" Bri asked in his soft tone of concern as he now sat at the corner of the bed.

"Like a cloud in a blue sky...peaceful!" Mia smiled. Her quirky sense of humor elicited a youthful vibe in Bri that tempered the serious, sinister side borne from years of street experience. Mia also planted a seed within Bri, one that moved him to cultivate and define the next phases of their interaction. Soon after, she would see Bri off to the airport, reinvigorated and motivated by her night's glowing and unforgettable first.

CHAPTER VIII

The Next Phase

For the next five years, Mia focused on her studies and internships with the Mayor's office with Zen-like single-mindedness. She completed her under-and post-graduate studies at Howard, preparing for the next chapter of her life's book, one she knew was hardly out of its prologue. A chapter in which was not written in any school's curriculum, a thesis that her experience would, in time, soon write. Her college years passed as mere days. Graduation day came and Mia stood on stage, valedictorian of her graduating class. No one was more proud than Savita, who watched her daughter from the auditorium's front row. To Savita, her husband's spirit was never more present than now. Savita's mind flashed pictures of Davis standing on the stage of Mia's eighth grade graduation. Pride for her daughter mingled with pride of her own for keeping her promise to Davis, that Mia would graduate college. Amongst the crowd of faces, Mia zoomed in on her mother, waving sensing the pride in Savita's smile. To her mother, she would always be Mia Flower, sitting at the window for hours late at night, waiting for her father to arrive from work. Melancholy washed over Mia, who'd have given anything for her father to witness this moment.

After the graduation caps had fallen from the sky, there stood Bri, heading Mia off before she got to her mother. He handed her an envelope, and discreetly kissed her on the cheek. Bri always took caution in public to not reveal the extent of their involvement. "Well, you've done quite well for yourself. Congratulations!" Bri said.

"Thank you for everything!" Mia responded. "Are you staying over the weekend?" she asked.

"Naww, I'm gonna catch a flight back home, I have some business to tend to. I just had to make it - you know I wouldn't have missed this moment!" Bri said of her graduation. When Savita finally spotted Mia in the crowd, Bri and Mia parted ways. Mia sat on the bleachers, excited to open up the envelope that Bri had given her. She opened the envelope and enclosed in a letter was five grand. Mia's jaw had dropped, never having held that much money in hand at one time. She looked for Bri through the crowd, to signal her thanks, to no avail. But the monetary gift would come secondary to the words he had written in the form of poetry.

I've walked here before, but there's an absence of a trace,

I've known this path, yet never traveled this way.

Ahh, there lay your footsteps as if I were without sight before!

I've seen the same stars a thousand times;

though differently cast in the reflection in your eyes.

Even the glow of the moon seems brighter.

As with the days, when even the sun seems more radiant, rising with her smile,

Only to set with the close of her eyelids.

Release me not into the lonely cells of darkness

That my heart dares to bear.

I'll stumble through the darkest wake of night if guided by your hand,

Before I'd walk the clearest path of the morning without.

Bri had titled the poem, "*Night of Dark's First Dawn.*" It was a literary commemoration of their first time together, Mia's first intimate experience. Mia was overcome by the depth of his words and his ability to convey such thoughts in that form. The reality, unbeknown to Mia, was that Bri had paid one of the workers at the club, a spoken word artist, who hosted poetry nights there, to write it. Judging by her reaction, Bri's final phase of wrapping her up was complete.

From a distance, Bri had assumed the de facto paternal role in Mia's life, playing an integral part in her educational pursuits. It seemed only befitting that he'd procure the fruits of his financial contributions over the years; only now Mia realized he'd been underwriting her education. These years saw them formalize their relationship, becoming a recognized social item. Mia's work in the Mayor's office made her a marketable commodity in the public relations and governmental affairs arena that dominated elite D.C. She was immediately offered an associate position with the lobbying department of Shalexa Governmental Relations. She had come to love this kind of work, and it was here that she hoped all the countless hours of studying in school would pay off. She was conflicted, however, because she also felt pulled to return home to St. Louis, to be with her mother, to connect with Bri in a more meaningful way. Bri understood her dilemna, but didn't want to overreach in trying to convince her to return. He didn't want to appear desperate and show his need. That would run counter to his goal of dominating her psyche. Bri called in a favor from an old associate, Irvin F. McCallister, who ran the most successful minority consulting firm in the city and Bi-State region. Mr. McCallister offered Mia an opportunity to work with his firm, making the decision to return to St. Louis more desirable – a job she yearned to try, and people she loved. Mia was oblivious to the inside social politicking Bri was using as a stratagem to keep her close. She received the formal job offer from Nord-Ellis and Milton Consultants, and overcome with enthusiasm, immediately called Bri to tell him the news and seek his input. "Heyyy, guess what? I got a job offer from Nord-Ellis and Milton." Mia said with excitement.

"Here in St. Louis? That's heavy baby!" Bri said feigning unfamiliarity. "So what you gonna do?" he asked.

"What you think?" Mia asked.

"I don't think I can be objective, because I would say Nord-Ellis, they're huge!" he said. "And I'm not saying that just because I wanna get close to you," Bri added jokingly. "Really! Well, I would have been totally flattered if that was your motivation!" Mia teased him.

Before she accepted the position, though, Mia thought it appropriate to inform her mentor, the one who had shaped her professional direction and given her the confidence to engage the public. Mia hesitated, because she knew that Mayor McNarry would be deeply disappointed. They had talked of moving Mia to a Cabinet-level position, a reasonable move since she'd worked as his protégé the last six years. Finally pushing pass her fear, she phoned the mayor. "Well, hello Mia, congratulations! Ready to take D.C. over?" he answered the phone with an expectant joke.

"Hey, Marion! I wanna say thanks for everything. You've opened
my eyes and given me an understanding and direction that I
would've never known without your guidance." Mia said somberly.

"Hey, it's been a pleasure watching you grow. You OK?" The
Mayor asked, sensing her reserve.

"I'm moving back to St. Louis to accept a position with Nord-Ellis."
Mia said, finally letting her breath go with a sigh. A long,
uncomfortable pause and silence preceded the Mayor's response.
"Hello, um, are you there?" Mia asked, hoping he hadn't dropped
the line.

"Yes, yes! Well. I'd be a liar if I said I'm not disappointed. But, I
guess you have to do what's best for you. I s'pose I'll have to hold
D.C. together myself!" His attempt at light humor softened any
anger in his tone. He grimaced on the other end of the line, though,
upset for both personal and professional reasons. He'd invested his
time and resources in something in which he now couldn't cash out
his vested interest.

His emotional stock market had crashed, dragging his mood down
with it. "Are you OK?" Mia asked.

"Yes, I'm fine. D.C. will always be here for you! Good luck, Mia,"
he told her, and hurried off the line before he said anything
unprofessional. McNarry figured that part of the reason for her
relocation was Bri. The mayor had long sensed that Mia was
smitten like a schoolgirl with Bri. Now, this Midwestern thug had
swept Mia right out from under him, and his ego was decidedly

bruised. Bri did not have the pedigree, the status, to deserve a prize like Mia. McNarry scowled and rubbed his now-throbbing forehead. This wasn't over. Mia returned to St. Louis to take the position at Nord-Ellis and Milton, and she and Bri began an exclusive relationship. Mia possessed an exotic beauty and the kind of intellect that gave Bri more credence in the public's view, which assisted him in more ways the one. Bri knew that beauty begets beauty, and Mia's presence drew many women to him, each one curious as to what was behind Mia's affection for him. His expensive lifestyle appealed to women whose main strength was beauty, but not a soul who really understood the life of a club owner would believe that his financial holdings, prime real estate, sleek cars, jewelry and luxurious vacations were funded by the success of a club operation. Neither did the Feds.

CHAPTER IX

Fall from Grace

Nearly two years passed as Mia worked tirelessly to climb the ladder at her consulting firm, finally branching off to form her own.

Even though she was back home, her intense commitment to the success of her business and her relationship with Bri put pressure on her friendship with Pam. Pam had continued to wander aimlessly, struggling to find stability in her personal life or any semblance of a professional career or job. She was the classic example of one whose reluctance to let go of the glorious, carefree party days of youth stymied her growth and the reality of a successful future. Still, she remained Mia's closest friend, and she entrusted confidences to Pam. Bri enjoyed nominal success in the club, found his deepening involvement in peddling dope far more lucrative.

Bri's condo in downtown Clayton was raided just hours after one of the biggest deals in the area, involving a fifteen-person drug ring that stretched throughout Southern Illinois and St. Louis, was exposed. Everyone connected to the ring was scrambling, as the Feds flipped culprits like flapjacks. The sentences were handed down harshly and quickly, ranging upward from thirty years to life.

Even knowing the consequences of snitching, especially against the Mexican cartel from Ciudad de Juarez, the majority of those busted took their chances and cut deals, instantly turning from hustlers into snitches. Bri cooperated and found himself sentenced to twelve years, snitching out on a plea, because thirty to life was too much to bear. Twelve years was obviously a sentence befitting one who had talked, but without a trail, Bri's cooperation with the federal government became legendary speculation on the streets. It was not enough for Big Red and the organization to distant themselves, although Bri still had to pay a hefty tribute. But his possessions – the cars, homes, the club and especially his status, in which he took great pride, were all reduced to a passing fancy. Most of his hangers-on had vanished. Those who had long eaten from the bounty of his mystery pursuits were now filling their bellies elsewhere, as Bri sat in the county jail, starved for what once was.

Mia was devastated. She had been independent of material want and absent of that which drove so many other young women outside what her own pursuits garnered. She wanted Bri for the person he was, not the picture of him being glorified on the streets. Bri understood all too well the social dynamic of relationships when one went to jail. Some hold...some fold. He wondered what his fate with Mia would be. He resolved not to fool himself into believing that any woman would walk that loyally, keeping himself from letting his heart desire or expect such. The marshals were shipping Bri from the county jail to the Federal Penitentiary in Forrest City, Arkansas in less than forty-eight hours. Mia would pay her last visit before his departure. Bri could not have been more wrong in his estimation of her love, loyalty and commitment. She was like Teflon, and no outside influence would stick. Mustering up enough positive energy to fuel a smile, she arrived in the visiting room to greet a waiting Bri. "Hey, babe!" she said.

"How you doin'?" Little emotion sounded in Bri's response. He found himself working through the early stages of steeling his emotions, deadening any attachment to the world that would soon become obscure.

"I'm holding. How about you, soldier?" she said brightly, hoping to raise his spirits.

"It is what it is!" Bri said.

"Wha, what does that mean? You ain't dead!" Mia said, attempting to offer strength at the same time, understanding where he was going in his mind.

"Look baby girl, I appreciate everything you've done and been to me. I got a Green Mile to walk, and it ain't fair to ask you to walk it, ya digg?" he said. His undetectable reverse psychology beckoned the opposite and desired response.

"Baby, no, I'm here. I'll hold it down. I'll walk the Green Mile and mow the MF!" Mia said, pleading like a child on the sidelines, waiting to prove herself in the game.

"Look, if you say you can soldier, then soldier. It's only one way to do that, loyalty in, loyalty out! You in the huddle or you're not!" Bri asserted. "'Cause baby, I'm gonna rebuild this army and make you a five-star general." He finally let slip a glimpse of a smile.

His words drew her awe, as if she were once again a teenage girl with a numbing crush. "Okaaay!" Mia responded with the softness of wet cotton.

"Time's up, visitation is over, please exit the VR!" the guard called. Bri returned to his cell, sitting, reflecting on the hurtful past his street activity and legal troubles hadn't afforded him the time to ponder; his father's death, his mother's struggles and ultimate demise.

69

It was as if the legend of his notorious father, D'Ray, was manifesting itself in Bri's own destiny as he sat, unable to escape the chains of his own DNA.

The Roots of a Hustler

Bri was born Brandon Baptiste in the Druid Hill section of Baltimore's Lower North Side, known as one of the East Coast's most crime-ridden, impoverished neighborhoods to Delray and Hattie Baptiste. His father, a Haitian immigrant who'd escaped the oppressive regime of dictator "Poppa Doc" Duvalier in 1959, had become legendary on the streets of Baltimore as a hustler, small-time heroin dealer and arms broker for street and government rebels in his native Haiti.

Delray was a charming man with deep pockets whose Haitian accent and notoriety made him all the more intriguing to the ladies. He managed to parlay their affection into a lucrative pleasure market. The launching pad for this venture was a storefront hole in the wall, a criminal one-stop shop enterprise. Pool hall, part club, part dope house, where one could peruse scantily clad women, an urban dungeon of the forbidden. One in particular, Hattie McCoy, an aspiring singer from Greenville, Mississippi, by way of Chicago's crime-laden Cabrini-Green projects, making her no stranger to the hustler and gangsta exploits of the streets. Hattie left the Midwest in the pursuits of the craft-friendly East Coast and settled in Harlem in an apartment atop of Marte's Shoe Shop on bustling 110th Street. A 5'5", thick redbone, Hattie had a Sarah Vaughn-esque voice, and Josephine Baker sex appeal, and she made it her policy to curry favor with whomever she thought could assist her in her quest for "stardom."

But Harlem was full of promise makers and dream breakers, and Hattie fell victim to Harlem's fast spin and all its trappings, until she found an escape from her own reality in heroin. Using her awe-inspiring sex appeal, Chicago street prowess and southern

71

Mississippi charm, she began turning high level tricks for industry professionals, club executives and even working the drug circuits for some of Harlem's most notorious kingpins, like Nicky Barnes and Frank Lucas. She'd have made a comfortable living if not for the heroin dependency that not only put her finances in the red, but her life. As the downward spiral of drugs and debt took its toll, Hattie was once more forced to escape the inevitable. She moved south, landing in Baltimore, which had begun to establish a reputation as Harlem-lite. By learning from her own mistakes, all the missteps that had led her through a haze of second-rate order-takers who tried passing themselves off as shot-callers. She developed a razor-sharp sense for BS, learning how to bypass the trial and error of "working" up the ladder, and go right to the top.

Keeping her antenna tuned to the street wave, she kept hearing reference to D'Ray, the name the streets had christened DelRay Baptiste. D'Ray's spot, the Blue Swan, was to Baltimore what the Cotton Club was to Harlem, but exclusively frequented by the hustler elite. Even the police who patrolled Precinct Six humbled themselves and understood that his establishment and its patrons were off-limits to heckling or harassment by any officer. Hattie set out to work the Swan, confident that she could work her way to D'Ray. Hattie equipped herself with a head turning arsenal of red and black tiger-print pencil-legged pants, four-inch patent leather pumps, and a top that hugged her 36Ds. She swayed into the Swan, an ocean of heads turning in her direction. She immediately sought to identify D'Ray and her search was short-lived. A bevy of women and two bodyguards dressed in all black surrounded the corner nook of the VIP area, a safe bet they were in D'Ray's orbit. Placing herself in his direct line of sight, she upped the ante. Stopping the waitress, "Excuse me, dear, what is that gentlemen's drink of choice?" Hattie asked. "Crown Royal on the rocks," answered the waitress. Hattie sent the drink with a handwritten note on a napkin…. "*YOU HAVE A QUALITY JOINT, FIT FOR A COMPLIMENT AND A DRINK. I'M HONORED,*" Hattie wrote. The cocktail waitress approached D'Ray with the drink and the note, "Mr. Ray, the young lady over there sends her regards." D'Ray broke in the midst of his conversation, obviously impressed by Hattie's style. He had no idea that she'd spent her last coins on the cab ride over and the drink. He motioned with a nod of his head for Hattie to join him.

The two ladies already draped over D'Ray, were none too happy to see his attention shift to Hattie. He could not deny her physicality nor hide an attraction. As any focused, successful hustler, he immediately identified opportunity and talent, and just how to fit it into his scheme. "Watit do for a lovely layydee like you?" D'Ray asked in his smooth French-Caribbean accent, grabbing her hand and pulling her to sit next to him.

"First, you should call me Hattie, and second, I believe I can do something for you," Hattie seductively offered.

"Like a whatta, layydee?" he asked.

"I can start by taking that 'Help Wanted' sign down," gesturing toward the window, "I'm all the help you need," Hattie held his gaze. Pausing, he thought that she'd be the perfect spider to cast a web for a cache' of sexual provocateurs; a critical piece to building his diversified cartel of drugs, gun trafficking and women…A crime trifecta.

Months passed with Hattie working the night shifts at the Swan.

Her presence caused a boom in business, as D'Ray sought to cement his investment and take her off the market. After her weekend shift ended, he knew it was now or never to secure Hattie's service, so he offered her a ride home. D'Ray ran his A-game in the back of his plush 1957 Cadillac. D'Ray even retrofitted the evening with her old pleasures to seal the moment…heroin and coke. "Listen bay, I do well for myself...by myself. But at some point in life you want to build with someone that you can trust. You and I can take Baltimore and ride this program up the East Coast," D'Ray said, as she sat like butter in his seat. "Can you ride, baybee?" he asked, so cool he made Superfly look square. He'd broken down more defenses that her street savvy could possibly prepare.

"Yes….yes baby, I gotchu," Hattie agreed, trying not to appear too anxious. D'Ray took his finger, running the course of her lips, thrusting it gently in her mouth. Then he held out the fore of his hand laced with a line of cocaine. "Let's ride!" Hattie said taking the bill he'd rolled for her. It was the sealing of their deal, her nose the ink upon the backseat contract. At that moment, in an instant, he had her locked in, in more ways than one. He'd circled her detour right back to the same exit she'd taken out of Harlem, but she didn't care.

It was here also that D'Ray got his first glimpse of the red-brick house, as he blazed inside of her until the windows fogged completely, his bodyguards standing watch outside.

From that night, his business reached seemingly endless peaks, as Hattie anchored D'Ray's ascent as one of the East Coast's top-tier hustlers. Nearly ninety percent of the heroin in the Baltimore and DC area flowed through D'Ray's operation. The lucrative side hustle in arms dealing underwrote the drug trade, and his cache of pleasure-fillers was growing as well, with Hattie as headmistress.

New Year's Eve, 1960. The Blue Swan's gala brought out the upper echelon of every social strata; sports figures, politicians, entertainers, hustlers, pimps and players from both ends of the coast. New York's up-and-coming Lucco Franks, strongman for Bumpy James, boxing great Sonny Liston, jazzman Thelonious Monk and emissaries from mob boss Sonny Bonnano's crew to South Florida's Jewish golden boy, tycoon Joey Friedman, storied to be the nephew of Meyers Lansky, were all on hand to celebrate. Some were there to taste the diversity and capacity of the East Coast's fastest growing criminal operation. Others wanted to gauge the strength of what might become a growing vine of competition that threatened to choke off their own criminal crops.

Noticeably absent was Hattie, herself as much a part of this success and growing legacy as D'Ray. She'd taken to her bed, praying that stomach flu was the culprit but knowing all too well the symptoms were more aligned with the morning sickness. Returning to Hattie's pad after such a dazzling display of the ripening fruits of his labors, D'Ray couldn't hide his disappointment. "Bay-bee, dis a big time, big game, waz de mada?" he asked, his tone tinged with an inkling of angst, as he knew Hattie wouldn't miss such a big night without a legitimate reason. Hattie all but knew she was pregnant and the nausea was worsened by the stress of knowing D'Ray wouldn't welcome the news. He was finally sitting on the high court of organized crime, now wasn't the time for distractions. Only death would stop his desire to reign over Baltimore and lay new grounds north to Manhattan.

The burden of raising a child would fall solely on Hattie. She understood this signaled her eventual fall from grace as the top thoroughbred in D'Ray's stable. She remained privy to the amenities and luxury he provided, yet it couldn't stop her from spiraling into depression five months into her pregnancy.

She confined herself to her home to protect D'Ray's rep and shield his private life. His desire to begin his coastal expansion forced her to up the ante. His travels back and forth to Haiti, supplying arms to street revolutionaries looking to overthrow the regime of "Poppa Doc" Duvalier, became more frequent, more dangerous, yet more lucrative. The increased revenue from the sale of guns would buoy D'Ray to the top of the drug trade by allowing him to buy in more volume direct from the poppy fields controlled by the junta leaders of Southeast Asia. But his ladder of success was abruptly cut down. In the seventh month of Hattie's pregnancy, D'Ray was killed on the streets of Port-au Prince by street loyalists of Duvalier.

Some wondered about the possibility of involvement by the Florida and New York crime syndicates, threatened by D'Ray's rise.

CHAPTER X

World Beyond the Wall

Bri sat in the holding cell at Forrest City's penitentiary, awaiting processing, reflecting on his past, the father he knew only through the legends of the streets, the mother he witnessed wither away to the cancer of the streets. He'd steeled his nerves to the controlled environment of jail hoping to distance himself from his emotional attachments to the outside. Mia, committed to walking the Green Mile even as Bri doubted she would, visited him every other week, riding down from St. Louis with spouses and girlfriends of other inmates. It was a distance that brought them closer, at least in Mia's mind. She was consumed by fulfilling her word. She held it down, rejecting overtures of physically intimacy and financial support from men who had waited in the wings to exploit the separation. Even as her commitment pulled Bri emotionally closer to Mia, he was, in many ways, becoming ruthlessly hardened inside, his thoughts zeroing in on his pursuit of the top.

He'd take advantage of the relationships in the pen. It was an environment full of men of means, like his bunkmate, Manuel Curtis, known on the inside as "Man Man," a venture capitalist and investment banker on the downside of a fifteen-year bid for bank fraud, tax evasion and wire fraud. Bri spent many days studying the trading markets, investment banking and general business concepts with Curtis. With each passing day, his old reality outside became a blur, his vision of future success gaining diamond-sharp clarity in his mind. For now, Bri's bank account and personal holdings lay decimated, emptied by his legal costs and federal for. Mia was his only connection to the outside, the only one he could trust.

He hoped that what he had invested mentally, physically and emotionally in Mia would eventually yield a financial return, enough underwrite his incarceration. Bri made thirteen dollars a month working in the kitchen, barely enough to shop for even the basic commissary necessities. So Bri hustled, selling eggs, chicken and cottage cheese he'd pilfer after his shift, and high demand, high-protein contraband among the inmates who worked out. Bri made inside connections with the commissary workers, allowing him to stockpile the most sought-after items; mackerels, tuna, honey, peanut butter and honey buns, and sell them for triple their value. Man Man set him up with the game, and it wasn't the money or the products he amassed that Bri coveted, but the power and notoriety that he gained, even behind the wall. This was instrumental in Bri maintaining a psychological edge. In this world, when his power didn't wane, all didn't seem lost. Every prisoner need, Bri positioned himself to provide. He eventually delved into smuggling in protein powders, contraband that was viewed the same as having a brick of cocaine in your possession, and cell phones. His criminal entrepreneurial pursuits knew no bounds, even in jail. Eventually, he amassed enough prison capital to venture in the direct drug trade and prostitution. These prison markets were controlled by a faction of the Mexican mafia called La Familia. They ran the drugs, and the prostitution and gambling were split between the Black Guerilla Family and the Aryan Brotherhood. Bri unwittingly began to undercut the Mexicans with his involvement in buying wholesale and selling retail, and this didn't sit well. These criminal activities fell within well-defined, governed markets and territories that worked in sync.

Any encroachment by one family into the other - BGF, AB or La

Familia - was met by extreme action, and Bri was growing in a sea of sharks. Manny, respected as an "underground ambassador" of sorts, often negotiating disputes, and calming one such potential conflict, was confronted by a lieutenant from La Familia. "Esa, your bunkie is out of bounds! If it don't stop, he got the heat coming from the AB and the Family....see what you can get DONE!" Bri was fortunate that the lieutenant and Manny had a close relationship; few were afforded the courtesy of a forewarning. Manny knew that crossing the AB or Mexicans meant not only death, but murder in the most grotesque manner, a message to anyone considering going into business on their own.

"Thanks, Papi! You know he's a young man, he's just not aware of the rules. I'll take care of it," Manny assured Gomez, unbeknownst to Bri, sparing his life for the moment. As Bri returned to the cubicle after his kitchen shift, Manny grabbed him, standing him up. "Look young blood, this ain't the Lou, Big Red ain't extended his hand here, so you gotta slow your road! The AB and La Familia breathin' down your throat, with the blessing of the BGF!" Manny said.

"I'm supposed to give up what I work for to some low-life criminal MFs?" Bri growled arrogantly. He appeared oblivious to the seriousness of the potential repercussions, not seeming to grasp the difference between his protected status on the St. Louis streets and the rules of a prison hierarchy.

"Young blood, you givin' up somethin' - it's either gonna be your work or your damn life! Now, I'm tryin' to make sure you make it out o' here to that fine-ass woman back home!" Manny nodded toward a picture of Mia on Bri's wall. "Ya figga digg me, young blood!" he added, as Bri stood stoically, yielding to the wise counsel of the one inmate he trusted.

"I digg!" Bri humbly responded. Manny went back to counsel with the AB, La Familia and the BGF captains to smooth things over.

But Manny was a businessman, and he knew Bri had a consumer following and was liked in the inmate market. This gave him a negotiation angle. He unilaterally negotiated a deal that gave Bri a quarter cut from the business he'd skimmed off their prostitution and heroin markets, turn the customers back to them and serve as an independent broker, of sorts, continuing to bring in business. They would leave him the lower level markets, like cell phones, protein supplements and food to Bri. This preserved his life and gave him an officially recognized, protected market niche. For his part, Manny got his ten percent direct cut, and hard products at no cost, without being on the hook for any of Bri's possible future indiscretions. Bri didn't know what to expect from Mia's first visit, which came several months into his stay. Word on the streets was that Mia had been seen around town frequently with a male business associate, a man Bri once cautioned her about. Bri had suspected him of many of the rumors that had dogged him prior to his incarceration, and possibly of cooperating with the Feds. He didn't allow this to get to him; one of the advantages of being able to steel his emotions, yet it did bother him. He couldn't open up to her after she'd allowed herself to be seduced by someone who worked against him. Their letters and conversations had been few and far between, as Mia worked to grow professionally and personally in Bri's absence. Buoyed by the confidence of the potential of his future pursuits upon his release, he had come to terms with the possibility of not being with her. Although others had volunteered to fill the void, Bri dismissed any potential companions, opting instead to focus on his master plan. Then Mia came to visit during an early spring weekend in April.

He had not seen her since leaving the St. Louis County Jail's holdover cell. Bri had remained, but as she walked through the visitation door, his skepticism subsided, as time and distance seemed to pronounce her beauty. Mia was equally as excited to see Bri, whose appearance was transformed. Bri walked toward her in his green uniform, nearly thirty pounds heavier with a full beard. "Hey there, lady!" Bri said with his voice deepened.

Bri paused for only an instant before reaching for her outstretched hands. Her eyes swelled with tears and her smile greeted him, "Heyyyy!" Mia said, at a loss for words as she rested her head on his shoulder. The visitation seemed to pass quickly, their time inundated with taxing conversation. Mia shared some of her challenges; she didn't know Bri was having her watched and thus already knew much of it.

Bri was at a comfortable place, having humbly submitted to his inability to impact anything on the outside. "Well, baby, I understand you got challenges - you do what ya need to do. I told you my day will come, I'll be alright. 'Memba,' everybody can't hold!" Bri said. Mia listened to a confident Bri, oblivious to where she now sat, in her decision to hold or fold. He had come to terms with what he already assumed to be the inevitable.

"You put me out there in these situations, you left me!" Mia shot back.

"Baby, I didn't volunteer to come to jail, but I gotta pay my dues. Sorry you were hit by all this, but you had a choice to stay or go. You still do." Bri said, calmly. "If you stay, I expect you to be true to your choice, and if not, then that's how it goes…but you can't have it both ways!"

"Well, I'm trying to understand…" Mia began to say as Bri cut her off.

"Look, I'm sitting behind these damn walls, can't do a damn thing. I'm acceptin' that. If you ain't gonna relieve the pressure, don't add none. Life's about choices. Make a choice and stand by it. I gotta go, time's up." Bri left the visiting room, leaving Mia perplexed. Bri knew how Mia had endeared herself to the young man, and the pressures of others who had attempted to come to the damsel in distress. He seemed to know she'd been questioning the value of holding for him, while others with more stable social and economic stations wanted to take over. Mia wanted Bri to bow to her decision to hold, to feel pain like he caused her by leaving her left alone. But Bri refused to go through what felt like another stage of a prosecution or persecution. He understood the impact of his actions, but no one else had to do a day of his time, without the options that freedom offered the critics. Bri preferred that she distance herself rather than stay and bring in the possibility of betrayal. It wasn't about jealousy, as Mia had assumed. Bri himself could have just as easily scored women with financial means and status on the inside or out. No, this was about him making a decision to trust someone, someone who then trusted and continued a working or personal relationship with someone they both knew meant him or their relationship no good. Whether personal or professional, the possibility of betrayal was like dead fish on a pile of crap, a stench he just couldn't stomach. His mind was at peace with all that his predicament brought, with that one exception. So he knew he had to get back to biding his time before his mind leapt to that irrevocable and deadly state of vengeance. Anyone he perceived to disrespect him, his family or operation could've easily been showered in the dark shadows of that vengeance, darkness worse than most could fathom. He tried not to go there. When he made it back to his dormitory, Manny asked, "How was the visit, Young Blood?"

"Well, it was ah ite. Can't stop my bid!" Bri said. Bri sat in his top rack, wanting to forego the next day's visit with Mia and avoid the grief. He didn't need any emotional roadblocks on the smoothest path as possible to his bid. To safeguard himself against the thought that Mia would ultimately let him down, he placed their connection in the freezer of emotional indifference.

Business on the inside was good for everyone, even the guards who benefitted from their role in the illegal activities, providing protection and safe entry for the goods. The agreement that Manny set up between Bri and the families had been mutually beneficial with no kinks. Not until Bri entered into a side deal with a new guard with whom he'd been chatting up for awhile. The guard talked of marijuana connections in Arizona. Bri rationalized that such a deal didn't violate the agreements with the families. Heroin was the drug of choice and abundance, and marijuana was scarce. The guard, who'd actually been contracted with the BGF, tipped them off to Bri's backdoor deal. Manny, who had been sent to the hole when he was subpoenaed to testify in another case, was anticipating a temporary transfer to another Federal holdover facility. Bri was left without his respected counsel, no one to intervene with the families on his behalf. The order had already come down from all the syndicates, and the Aryan Brotherhood agreed to fill theprescription.

Bri worked the mid-shift in the kitchen. That evening, the guards conveniently locked the exits and disappeared to answer a disturbance elsewhere on the yard. As Bri was taking the dumpster of trash out the rear exit, two white inmates, with the numbers 88 tattooed on the sides of their heads, approached Bri. Bri knew all of the kitchen personnel, and these two he had not seen. He knew they were Nazi-Aryan sympathizers. The number 88 symbolized Heil Hitler, representing the eighth position of the letter H. "Hey, Nigger! You eatin' out the dumpster now? What, the commissary ain't accepting food stamps, boy?" The two tattooed rednecks sneered as they confronted Bri. "Look here, you cartoon clowns, why don't I give you two dollars to go buy a condom, and go do what you do best…screw yourselves!" Bri retorted. The kitchen was the most dangerous place to get cornered, often locked with knives and weapons easily accessible. The two inmates exposed a shank made from carved toothbrushes, bound by nails and the lids of tuna fish cans. As they moved toward him, Bri knocked over a tall rack of gallon food containers into their paths. They gave chase as Bri jumped over the counters into the dish room, where he was finally cornered. Bri had drawn blood from the eye of one of the men, from a can that fell from the rack that he'd pushed over. "What's up now, Nigger? Why don't we take that condom you talked about and stick up your ass, boy?" The rotten-toothed, tattooed-covered Neo-Nazi said, as they both laughed.

Bri figured this was it, there was no use screaming, he would at least dignify his exit with the strength of a brave, fallen soldier. Throwing his hands up, "Well, do what you gotta do, you Nazi-racist dogs!" he said.

As the men began their rush toward Bri…"Hold up! It ain't goin' down like that, not today!" A burly, 6'5", three hundred pound Black man named Knuck emerged from the shadows of the kitchen, standing in the doorway watching the scene. "Look, this came down on high! The BGs signed off, so move yer ass!" the Aryan soldier said.

"Ah ite, I'll move - if you trailer trash, hog-eatin', fly-fishin' faggots can move me!" Knuck said, as five more giant Black prisoners made their way into the kitchen scene. "Like I said, BOY - not today, not today!" Knuck said, and the AB soldiers left Bri alone. Knuck and his crew were not with the BGF, but they occasionally muscled up and worked in conjunction if needed. They were considered the conscious, independent brokers of the jail, and garnered much respect. They had a disdain for the ABs, and always questioned the coordination with the BGF and them. Knuck had negotiated pulling the kill order on Bri by appealing to the Black consciousness of the BGF, and extolling Bri's usefulness, what with his outside connections and obvious knack for hustling on the inside. Bri could only muster a breathless, "Bro, thanks!"

"Listen, you broke code and in this game you don't even have ONE time. I only did this 'cause I respect Manny, and he liked you and I see something in you....I've negotiated you out the game!" Knuck said.

"It's done! Whatever, I'm out. Thanks, man!" Bri said. Although physically intimidating, Knuck was not the most physically attractive sight. He came into the prison system as a fourteen-year-old kid, never having had the touch of a woman. Bri found a way to repay him by using his cache' of beautiful women on the outside. They would pay a visit and break Knuck off a piece every once and again, through extended x-rated visitation sessions, during which they also handsomely "blew-warded" the guards for their silence.

Needless to say, the friendship grew between Bri and Knuck.

Knuck protected Bri's interests, providing him peace of mind and some security. Months went by with Mia and Bri only occasionally dropping a note or a call. As time passed, their distance apart intensified Mia's desire to go the distance with Bri. Most of the glitz and glam put forth by potential suitors still fell short of the voltage of the electrical current she felt with Bri. Bri, himself, was fine, even without the direct hand of Big Red behind his jailhouse pursuits.

He understood that when you're pinched, there's a need to create distance between associates. Plus, his legal troubles had been outside of the scope of Big Red's blessings, so alienation from the causes and effects was expected.

The Grass Outside the Walls

Although having had expressed her commitment and intention to hold it down, Mia still found herself weary from the time and distance and vulnerable to social interaction with men. She struggled not to only maintain, but first find an identity independent of Bri. First subtle, then pronounced, changes appeared. Her attire was more relaxed; she'd gone from Famous & Barr to Nordstrom's, from Anne Klein to Dior. Mia was not the socialite, at least not since becoming entrenched in her relationship with Bri and her career, but she began frequenting more social venues and events. The lines of professionalism were increasingly blurred between her personal interactions with male associates, all of whom provided a sense of comfort and security in a world absent of Bri. And that comfort was the wedge, opening her up to a fragile vulnerability. She embraced a new found sense of freedom without the responsibility of a relationship; a freedom that combined her vulnerability and inner conflict about a future with Bri, endeared her to her male associates. Bri knew the spin well – he understood and was completely powerless to stop it. In the midst of late-night meetings and business lunches with the taint of intimacy, Mia began to sense that the social bearings she was now guided by were leading her into straits of nothingness, relationships that would only temporarily fill the void of comfort. In the long run, Mia knew that such intimacy, mental or physical, would yield her nothing but as Bri would always say… a nut and a heavy heart. As much as things had come full circle from the first time she met Bri after prom to reconnecting with him after college, she had come back around with the surety of a heart set in stone.

Communication between Mia and Bri became more frequent, as well as her visits. She recommitted herself fully to their relationship. She had increased her workload to not only busy herself from male distractions, but also to support Bri during his imprisonment, and create a stable environment for him when he returned home. This was important because by this time, Bri had been cut off from his main sources of income, pushed out by the AB, La Familia and the BGF gang factions from his gambling, smuggling and drug running rings. But he'd begun making the most of his time, connecting to influential people in ways you couldn't find in any networking session. Inside, he had access to some of the great minds of banking, finance and business, to lawyers and doctors - a whole field of intellectually rich properties from which he could amass a wealth of knowledge and contacts. Nearly eight and a half years had passed since he'd entered the pen, These years saw Mia start her own successful consulting firm and acquire her own real estate, placing her in a financially comfortable position. The relationship endured as the months had turned to years, and Mia's dutiful commitment left Bri with no logical reason to deny her the honor of becoming his wife. In his eyes, she had proven worthy, and of course any good cost-benefit analysis would show it was clearly in his favor to do so. Mia beautiful, smart, accomplished, and had a credit rating that could lease the White House. Mia didn't care that Bri was a liability on paper. She'd longed to cement their relationship, and marriage was the most legitimate way. Her friends who were privy to her desire to marry him counseled against it. Her mother, who had never cared for Bri or his suspect lifestyle, abhorred the very thought. But the more they pushed against him, the more intense her affection for him grew.

Bri consulted with the prison chaplain and set up a marriage ceremony. Mia and Pam, who had remained silent in her opinion and outwardly indifferent, traveled to the prison for the wedding. Pam managed to withhold her envy from Mia for the entire trip. Bri was accompanied by Manny, who had long since returned from his transfer to Florence, Colorado's federal facility. Bri's dress green prison uniform was neatly pressed, his shoes shined like the glass outside a Windex factory. He wore eyeglasses, which gave him a softer, intelligent look that Mia simply adored. She changed into a white lace dress that draped off her shoulders, hugged her hips and swayed perfectly at the bottom, barely kissing the floor. Their ceremony was jointly performed by the chaplain, and Imam Seifullah Hayes, a man for whom Bri had much respect and admiration. It was the Imam, whom Bri had never met in person, who commissioned Knuck to intervene on his behalf with the Aryan Brotherhood and save his life.

Bri and Mia exchanged their vows. Mia's smile was reminiscent of the one she wore that long-ago morning after making love with Bri at the Hay-Adams in D.C.

Once they were married, Mia, with the help of some of Bri's inside financial connections, purchased a home in affluent Huntleigh Manor, a hilly suburb with winding streets and mansions set behind lush landscaping. Bri vowed to get on top of his game and Mia put her complete love, belief and trust in him – much to the chagrin of her friends and family. Bri was finally up for early release after serving ten years of his twelve year bid. With a strong recommendation from the chaplain, the educational resource officers, and Bri's spotless personnel record, his petition for release into a Probation Pre-Release Program was approved. The program would allow him twelve months of residential stay in a halfway house, and six months home confinement. He would be released nearly eighteen months early; and Mia couldn't have been more excited.

Mia secured their home, provided a new wardrobe and placed him on her official payroll to fulfill the job requirement of probation. Bri moved quickly to position himself back into street relevance and establish financial self-sufficiency. He had convinced Mia to purchase a building so he could re-open a club, and he immediately leveraged the equity in the building to purchase a new Mercedes-Benz. Mia thought this was too quick. She knew enough about the Feds to know they'd keep a watchful eye on every dime, every purchase, but Bri managed to circumvent the watchful eye of Probation and Parole and the Feds on all fiscal movement by making purchases and investments through Mia, and partnerships in which he remained silent. In light of the hefty six-million dollar fine he owed the federal government, he thought this best. No risk, all reward was how Bri built his empire before, and he was determined to build it back up again. Having all the pieces in place, including the funding and venue, he found himself missing only one thing. He needed a political inside to navigate the bureaucracy of City Hall and the various state agencies that handled every area of his business.

CHAPTER XI

The Roots of Ty

Ty was an attorney whose Harvard education belied his blue collar roots. Born Tyson Sheldon Penn in St. Louis, Missouri, he grew up to become a perfect mix of charm, chivalry, cunning and cool, his persona an outgrowth of his humble, inner-city, blue-collar upbringing. These traits allowed him to move and operate through any social strata and endeared him to a socio-political and economic cross-section of folks: doctors, lawyers, politicians, gangsters, dealers and hustlers. Quietly, Ty garnered a reputation as a well-connected, well-liked playmaker and connector. Bri witnessed this first-hand, learning fast in hopes of putting Ty's talents on reserve for future benefit. Manny, Bri's cellmate, best man and a former investment banker and venture capitalist, orchestrated their initial meeting. Manny had financed Bri's failed land assemblage scheme that nearly bankrupted the unincorporated area of Upland Park, hundreds of acres of barren land and dilapidated homes, and Ty's connections in the political and legal world proved invaluable. Bri ran into some bureaucratic red tape recovering money frozen in some offshore accounts in the Seychelles Islands. He wanted to develop a state-of-the-art, thirty-five-thousand square foot converted warehouse into the Mecca of nightclubs. It was classic Bri, doing it large at any cost. The two met at the Coffee Cartel Shop in the Central West End, both out of their normal elements.

Ty claimed himself to be a student of people, listening attentively, deciphering character flaws leaking through their words. He approached the suave Bri, and before he could sit down, "Ty, brotha, how are you? I heard a lot about you, they say you're the man, there's a lot…" Bri fired off a string of flattering musings before Ty cut him off, holding up his hand. Ty's humility made that much adulation, rife with patronizing puffery, almost painful. Much of what he accomplished was without effort, as his relationships with those of means were merely reflections of his affability, and the favors he pocketed were extensions of such.

"I've been blessed with good relations and I'm always willing to help. And a friend of Romel is a friend of mine." Ty said, referring to Romel Watts, another mutual acquaintance. Romel was a young man of like stature; street cred, an extensive social network of ballers, businessmen, politicians and music industry personnel. As Ty sipped his coffee, Bri explained his dilemma. Ty assured Bri he would do what he could. His cool confidence gave Bri hope. Parting ways, the two shook hands. But Bri's quick, superfluous talk gave Ty pause. The thought occurred to him that Bri might be wearing a wire; Ty dismissed that thought and moved forward to allow a relationship to form, accepting an invitation to meet the next evening at Bri's manse. Ty was conflicted by Bri's persistent overtures and gratuitous show of appreciation, but his concern was overridden by the burden of the student loan debt he'd amassed over four years at Boston University and three years at Harvard Law, not to mention the mortgage on his newly acquired Midtown loft. To quell his reservations, Ty phoned Romel. "What's up, Mel, what's the line on this Bri cat?" he asked.

"Listen, Bro, watch them all, trust no one but your mother, and keep one eye on her!" Romel warned Ty of Bri. That evening, he set out to visit Bri at his home in Huntleigh Manor. While not one moved by the material wealth of others, Ty still marveled at the neighborhood and its picturesque landscapes. The front entrance to

Bri's home was Romanesque, balanced by colossal marble columns, with ponds on both sides of the entryway. Ty reached for the doorbell; Bri startled him opening the door, warmly greeting him. "My brother, welcome. Come in please." Bri said, escorting Ty into a sitting room adorned with a mix of African art and Italian paintings, including a Picasso original. Bri seemed relaxed, wearing a red silk smoking jacket with a white velvet collar, and soft Italian leather loafers. He offered Ty a drink. "I'm here to serve you my brother, what's your poison?" he asked. "Tonic seltzer and cranberry," replied Ty, as he leaned back on the couch, admiring the vaulted ceilings and towering open glass elevator.

As the two immersed themselves in their business, Ty tuned out Bri's words when, in the corner of his eye appeared a vision more beautiful than anything he had ever seen. Mia Farone, Bri's wife. Mia was a tall, sultry figure with a petite and curvaceous body. Ty, ever conscious not to be disrespectful or covetous of another man's woman, quickly refocused his attention back on the conversation with Bri. Mia was visibly irritated and disengaged, but shifted her obvious irritation to an obligatory smile of courtesy. "Good evening!" Mia said, extending her greetings to Ty. He had to battle the natural urge to compliment such beauty, knowing he must show deference to Bri and the business at hand. As their conversation progressed, Ty wondered to himself why Bri had invited Mia into the conversation in the first place.

Bri slid Ty a stack of one hundred dollar bills. "This has nothing to do with anything; just my way of saying I appreciate our newfound friendship!" Bri said. Ty wondered silently why Bri intentionally conducted this in front of his lady. He rationined it as Bri's way of lowering the esteem she would possibly have of the younger Ty.

93

Mia sat motionless, observing the two exchanging handshakes as Bri escorted Ty out the door. She rolled her eyes and clinching her jaws in disgust, struggling to find the words to express. "I don't get you, Bri! You're throwing money around like we just got it like that!" Mia exploded. This was rare; she normally acquiesced simply for the sake of peace.

"I guess I don't know what the hell I'm doing now, but seems your ass is sittin' here livin' the high life off what I *'don't'* know!" Bri's voice trembled violently as he fired back. The exchange left Mia feeling grossly unappreciated, as if her efforts of helping build Bri up had vanished. Mia was never one to bring up her own generosity, but Bri had taken her out of her natural form. "Nigga, who held you down the last ten years? These may be your ideas, but your ideas have cost ME!" Mia wound up like a roaring engine. "That 550 out there? You ain't put so much as a gallon of gas in it!" seethed Mia.

Bri realized this unfamiliar emotional chord he'd struck with Mia was rooted in truth and steeped in her hurt.

It was a truth he kept hidden behind his self-centered ego. Mia's frustration and agitation made her pretty face look older and more worn than it really was. Hurt, she reflected upon all those years she'd soldiered on, true by his side, through his trial and time in the penitentiary. A feeling of despair settled in followed by an immediate and overwhelming sense of liberation. With the certainty of a DNA test, Mia resigned herself to the reality that she was an expendable pawn in Bri's game, nothing more to him than a beautiful showpiece to adorn his arm.

This harsh reality was liberating and sobering at the same time. A hangover of hurt pounded in her head as she sat on her bed, her thoughts cast back to Tivoli and her father. A world away it seemed, but tonight it felt closer.

Shadows over Tivoli

Don Carmine Lucci's years had cursed living with his wife, whose heart had died in the flames with her lover, Davis Whitmore. Don Carmine's remorse was uncharacteristic of a mobster; murder was justified by the mob code for taking up with a made man's wife. But with time, age and wisdom, he'd grown to see the true essence of that not governed by street or mob code. The Farone-Whitmores had never faded from the minds of many in the Lazio neighborhood of Tivoli, where Mia and his own Nadia had appeared together like conjoined twins. He and Vitalia were reminded of Davis's tragic fate every time they looked into the eyes of their daughter. Don Carmine wondered incessantly how Mia had made out since the loss of her father. Nothing much had changed in Tivoli – Don Carmine still held legendary sway and esteem throughout Tivoli and Rome, but his involvement in running the affairs of the family's enterprises had lessened. Vitalia knew that Davis's death had soured Don Carmine's desire to run the family. He ultimately began preparing his son, Carlo, to take over. Carlo was fifteen years Nadia's junior; born shortly after Davis died and his family left for the United States. The Luccis never talked of Davis, Savita or Mia; too many hurts and painful memories for both - Vitalia's infidelity and Davis's disappearance loomed over their relationship like a thunderhead, even though Tivolian authorities never established murder as the cause of death. That which bound Don Carmine and Mia over the miles was Tivoli of the loss of one another's family and a desire to one day meet.

CHAPTER XII

The Vines of Ty

Ty seemed to be everything to everybody. His concern and compassion often lead him to provide legal services without charge, and he often loaned his expertise in consulting and leveraging the political relationships of which he was privy. Those who knew Ty understood his motivation; he did it because he could; helping made him feel good. Generosity was rooted in his core. His father, Larry Ellis Penn, had been a giving, compassionate man who used his energies to help empower people, and his money to enhance charitable causes and community service. Although Ty worked the legal sector by profession, on-the-job training and mentoring he received from his father, who was versed in the backdoor mechanics of politics, organization and power, gave him his uncanny ability to maneuver and connect in those circles. Ty's political involvement long preceded who he saw as political neophytes who relished their titles but provided nothing of substance as they suffered a general lack of understanding of power and empowering others. His father was a hero Ty feared, loved and respected, and who later became a friend and confidante.

At the height of Ty's career he felt trapped on a hamster wheel, constantly spinning while stuck in one place. When the wheel suddenly stopped, his life jerked into sharp focus. The man he loved with a child-like adoration passed before his eyes on an unseasonably warm November morning. Ty, the middle son of five boys, had already served three years in his own prison of sorrow after the losses of his brother, Lamar, to cancer, his older brother

Simeon, an Army ranger, to the war in Afghanistan, and Bryant, to an actual fifteen-year prison sentence. Lawrence Jr. was the only brother left. L.J. was Ty's only connection to normalcy, tucked away from the fast, mean underbellies of law and politics. Behind Ty's broad smile and sanguine demeanor burned a numbing pain, unbeknownst to most, including his family. In some ways, his work and sacrifices in the community shielded him from the worst of it as the work forced his focus. After the memorial services for his father, Ty found himself at PF Chang's, open only to the lone company of whoever sat at the bar. He rarely indulged in alcohol, but the pain and loneliness of his father's death begged for the release of an elixir. Ty released himself from the reservations of drinking, ordered a glass of wine and lost himself in memories of his childhood days and his father. The rich, creamy *Clos du Bois* Chardonnay bit his lips like a December morning frost, then warmed his senses like a country fireplace. Although comforting to his senses, the alcohol thrust Ty further into his sorrow.

Mia Farone sat just a few feet away at a booth just outside the view of the bar with Pam. They still occasionally went out, but Mia had veered off the beaten path of the club scene and crowds, opting for more subdued and intimate venues. "You got me all the way in Richmond Heights?! You know I don't swing like this!" Pam laughed, as she pointed her chop sticks at Mia.

"Sometimes you have to change your pace," Mia replied, waving her hand at Pam, and they sat talking for hours. Pam, as usual, shared her updates from the rumor mills and of her own problems.

"Girl, guess who did…," Pam began, but Mia cut her off.

"I'm not goin' to even let you get started, girl. I've got my own problems and no space for nobody else's!" Mia told her firmly.

"Well, excuse me, Miss Thang!" Pam tossed back. "So what's your issue? Bri still got that whip working?" Pam joked.

"Whatever. I'm just tired," Mia sighed. Mia continued to pour out her problems, but Pam's attention was constantly diverted away from the conversation as she answered a string of text messages while Mia talked.

A cell phone blurted DJ Quick's "*B*@ch" Betta Have My Money*," and Pam jumped up. "Oh, damn, 'scuse me, girl - I gotta take this!" And she walked away from the table to take the call.

Mia watched her, fighting down disgust and shame. Shaking her head, she wondered if Pam was ever going to grow up.

"Ah ite, girl, I gotta go!" Pam said, packing her purse to leave.

"OK, be safe. Call me later?" Mia said, feeling relief at Pam's exit. Although two hours had passed, Mia was reluctant to cut her night short and go home. Home had become like a hotel; nothing more than a place to lay her head. Their foundation of love had crumbled, leaving nothing but a few bricks and crumbling mortar surrounding the two.

A Chance Meeting

Walking to PF Chang's exit, she suddenly detoured, opting instead for a cocktail at the bar. She sat at the furthest end opposite Ty, who continued tumbling between happy reminiscence to the painful loss of the present. Mia herself was steeling herself for another evening in the day-to-day peace initiative freezing the Cold War between her and Bri; brought about only by her commitment to honoring her vows. "What can I get for you ma'am?" the bartender asked Mia.

"Hmmm, let me see. Do you have Mosel-Saa-Rower Riesling?" she asked.

"No ma'am," he answered. "May I suggest the Marco Negri Moscato? It's got a light texture with just a hint of honeysuckle and rose," he suggested to Mia.

"I'll try it!" she agreed.

The bartender headed over to tend to Ty, who caught a glimpse, as if he recognized her. He focused his skewered vision and realized it was Mia. "What is she drinking?" he asked the bartender.

"Moscato," He answered.

"I'll pick it up!" Ty told the bartender, who strode back to Mia with her drink.,

He waved off her credit card. "Compliments of the gentleman at the end of the bar," he said with a smile. When Mia turned his way, Ty raised his glass in a distant toast. Mia reciprocated his toast, mouthed "thank you," and sipped her wine with a tiny smile.

Moments later, she climbed from her stool and made her way to Ty. "Thank you again, umm…" she failed to recall his name.

"Tyson Penn. But just call me Ty. And you're welcome." he nodded.

Mia turned then paused, sensing Ty's heavy mood. "Are you OK? That doesn't look like your regular tonic and cranberry." Mia smiled, remembering the drink Ty had enjoyed in her home with Bri.

"Ah, I'm good. I, uh, I lost my dad, just trying to clear my mind," Ty said. Without invitation, Mia sat down next to him. At a loss for words, she connected with his sorrow through her own paternal loss years ago. Ty rambled on softly about his dad, about random things Mia didn't understand.

"Hey, no one knows how you feel but you, but I can relate. I lost my father, too," she told him gently. An hour passed, as Mia's presence pulled him back from his emotional lull. The Moscato had taken a toll on Mia's stoicism, and she opened up on her childhood in Italy, verbal musings she rarely shared with anyone else. They swapped heartwarming stories about their fathers until the bar held no one else but the two.

The bartender walked toward the lone pair, but they knew it was past last call. "OK, OK, we know! Got to go…" Ty said as they both laughed and headed for the door. In just hours, the drinks and shared experiences of loss warmed the connection between them and, familiarity lingering. "Well, Mrs. Baptiste, thanks for the company," he said.

"Likewise, I appreciated it as well. And it's Farone, Mia Farone," Mia corrected him firmly. He took notice of her quick disassociation from her marital name.

Men hone in on the slightest body movement or sound to gauge how a woman feels about a personal matter, looking for hints about the state of their relationships. Ty let Mia's musings and her lack of connection with Bri fly over his head, blowing it off to the effects of the alcohol. "Well, goodnight," Ty said softly.

"Goodnight," Mia answered, as the valet pulled up with her car. Before pulling away, she rolled her window down. "Hey, if you're not doing anything, why don't you stop by the club this weekend? You might just enjoy yourself!" Mia offered.

"I might just do that!" Ty nodded. "Please give your husband my regards," Ty said waving goodbye.

Mia thought to herself, "I'll be damned if I tell him anything." Mia was so beautiful that Ty couldn't help but notice, but still, he wasn't one to peck around another man's nest, especially if it conflicted with business. But between the glasses of wine and conversation, his attraction to Mia had coalesced into something he couldn't ignore. Days passed, and Ty rented her more space in his mind than he'd ever imagined he would. He looked for an opportunity to take her up on the offer to visit the club.

CHAPTER XIII

Pandora's Box

Ty had familiarized himself with her Italian background. He gathered from their conversation at PF Chang's that Mia fostered an unyielding love of everything Italian. He'd even taken a self-study crash course in conversational Italian, during which his own appreciation of the language was peaked. He subsequently immersed himself in the study. His not-so-subconscious desire to impress and flatter Mia the next time he saw her fueled his concentration.

Saturday night was the busiest night at Club Movado. It was one of the few clubs in the area that catered to adult club-goers, a jazzy spot with a comfortable, upscale juke joint feel. Mia's typical post was in Movado's ritzy VIP area, where family, close friends and local dignitaries lounged in comfort. She worked back and forth, watching the money and greeting guests. Vintage bottles of 1974 Montaigne Chouteau lined the tables where her friends gathered, grabbing the immediate attention of everyone entering the club. Ty finally decided he'd pay a visit. He figured he'd talk to Bri while he was there; no one needed to know that business was not behind his visit. Ty entered and reached for his wallet. Bri saw him come in, and signaled to security to let him in, bypassing the scan and admission. "What's up, brother? I'm surprised to see you here!" Bri said.

"Hey, had to check what everybody else around town is talking about!" Ty shot back, as they traded hugs.

"Ah ite, well they didn't lie, this is where it's at!" Bri said, motioning to the bar. He ordered the staff to take care of his special guest and sent Ty to the VIP section. Ty sat, scanning the club, finally locking in on Mia, who headed toward him. Ty rarely lacked confidence, but his cool was temporarily thawed by her beauty and the soft aura floating around her approaching sway. Her Vera Wang strapless dress accentuated every curve, draping over red Dior Celeste t-strap platform pumps and exposing the fresh pedicure on her delicious toes. The moment veered into awkwardness when their gazes intersected. Mia's dimpled smile invited his approach, but Ty was a man of modest means, reserved demeanor, and subdued style. His style stood in stark contrast to Bri, known for his lavish taste in expensive tailored suits, Italian shoes, and luxury cars. Bri's popularity was derived from his familiarity with many of the Midwest's most successful hustlers and club owners. Mia's friends were no less opulent, as Bri's connections encouraged relationships of status and means. Bri was a Rolex and Ferragamos to Ty's Timex and Kenneth Coles.

Ty's elementary Italian served as a coded language, subtly underscoring his interest in Mia and flattering her all at once. Later, their shared language would serve to circumvent her friends and isolate Mia in conversation; the suspense of which merely broadened the attraction. "Buonsera! Il tuo belleza semplice!" Ty greeted her, sharing how beautiful he thought she was. His wine had served its social lubricant purpose, opening up his typically subdued approach. Even his thoughts translated in Italian, as he wondered silently, wanting desperately to say, "Io volere tu!...I want you!"

Mia held her composure, but was completely enamored with Ty's bold, romantic, coded advance in her native tongue. She tilted her glass, lowering it from the apple-red lips that complimented her pumps.

She didn't want to appear too forward or cross the lines of propriety; Ty was still a business associate of Bri. But she couldn't deny that their brief encounter had stoked her interest in talking with him even more. As Mia closed the memorable night, which moved along just at the speed of thought the fog of uncertainty met the sun on the horizon of certainty. No guessing needed to know the attraction was mutual; from the first glasses of wine to the cunning sensuality of their Italian exchanges, their desire was clear. From this night on, the occasional use of Italian added intrigue and excitement every time they met.

Many nights had passed since that one, nights that got continually heavier for Mia under the mounting pressures of debt, Bri's verbal abuse, his philandering and blatant disrespect. He treated her as if he owned her, pulling his acts from a pimp's repertoire. The burden wore down the Afro-Italian belle whose beauty had enamored so many, including Ty.

Ty had also borne the burden of abuse, still haunted by the soiled memories of the verbal, mental and physical abuse of his own sisters; he drew upon himself the ire of the mistreatment any woman he knew suffered. Prompted by that thought and his growing desire, Ty decided to give Mia a call. Her ringing phone signaled the end of a round in the prize fight that had become her marriage. Wiping her tears, she saw Ty on her caller ID. Easing away from her still ranting husband, Mia closed herself in the bathroom to take Ty's call. "Hey lady, how are you?" he asked.

"I'm ah ite. I'm jus' so damn tired! What're you doing later?" Mia whispered.

Ty sensed her tense frustration, relieved only slightly by the sound of his voice. With the boldness of a Vegas high roller, he gambled. "Can you step out? Don't say no - the Moscato is on me!" Ty said.

The pause felt like an eternity, but finally she whispered, "Yeah... yeah, I can do that. Where?" With the subdued excitement of a recently acquitted defendant, Ty suggested they meet at Kiener Plaza downtown at 7:45 p.m. sharp.

Escape to Kiener

Kiener Plaza resembled a smaller modern day Roman Coliseum. Its free-flowing fountains and descending steps circled the outdoor atrium, rounds of steps that doubled as seats. The 640-foot Gateway Arch was a perfect backdrop, towering over the historic Old Courthouse, a picturesque setting fit for a postcard. Ty knew that their meeting time would correspond with the setting of the sun. He recalled Mia mentioning she could not remember the last time she'd actually watched the sun set. The evening's weather was a perfect convergence of summer and fall, as the warmth was cooled by the kiss of a light breeze of wind. She approached Ty from behind, surprising him, strumming her fingers playfully across his neck. "Hey, stranger!" she said, her sensuous smile weakening his inner core.

"Heyyy! What's up? I thought you couldn't be out after the sun went down!" Ty teased her.

"Yeah, OK! I'm a good girl. I think I can hang out!" she joked back. Ty felt comfortable with her, as if they'd surpassed the suspended emotions of the platonic stage.

He embraced her, chancing the moment with a kiss on her cheek, strategically near her ear where his breath gently grazed her ear lobe. He led her to sit down. "There's your sunset," Ty whispered, gesturing toward the sun. Speechless, Mia closed whatever distance was left between them, edging closer and placing her hand on his thigh. Turning to her, Ty stared into her eyes. "Let's walk. What's your curfew?" he asked.

Ty joked, yet he seriously wondered how much time he would have with her. As they walked, Mia playfully nudged him along the way, prodding him to let her know where they were going. "Come on, where we goin'?" she asked. "OK, I see you're gonna be a tough one to surprise," he said.

"Well, maybe if I was used to them, I might be more patient," she replied. They finally stopped at the corner of Broadway and Market to sit on the steps of the Old Courthouse.

As they sat, chatting, a white carriage with red velvet interior, pulled by a well-coiffed Clydesdale, stopped at the intersection in front of them. "Wow, that's beautiful, reminds me of my hometown, Tivoli!" she said excitedly.

Mia reminisced about her last ride to the airport, when she, her mom and her dad had ridden in a horse-drawn carriage across Tivoli's cobblestones and dirt roads. Ty, always mindful of the smallest, yet sentimentally important details, had known it was exactly twenty years ago to the day that she left Italy for America, a fact that had not even registered with Mia herself.

Stepping from the carriage a distinguished gentleman rolled a red swath of carpet to the courthouse steps where Mia sat. Appropriate, because Mia had removed her shoes. Casting his hand to Mia, the escort smiled, "Mia Farone, per favore endare Ty la onore?" He asked, would she please do Ty the honor. "Si!" Mia answered softly, glancing at Ty with an astonished nod of deep pleasure and approval.

Inside, she marveled at Ty's meticulous display – a bottle of '68 Chateau de Montaigne, a rare vintage he'd had shipped directly from the vineyards of Bordeaux and the year of her birth. They were oblivious to any activity outside their carriage. The night offered the perfect warmth of 72 degrees, ideal for an outdoor escapade. Inside the carriage, a fresh bouquet of roses, violets, and stargazer lilies lay at her feet. Candles flickered with the scent of jasmine and lavender, flames dancing through the sparkle of their wineglasses. As the carriage rolled from the curb, the curtains dropped, providing complete privacy, and, as if on cue, Janet Jackson's "Anytime, Anyplace" began to play.

Before they could raise their glasses in toast, the moment itself intoxicated them. Every inch of Mia's senses were aroused, the Chateau de Montaigne removing any reservation, ushering in the moisture between Mia's limbs that only she knew, but Ty was soon to explore. She reached for his thigh, finding his mountainous peak instead. The lay of Mia's blouse accentuated the full perk of her nipples, and Ty's desire was so intense that his mouth began to water. Pushed to the very edges of her vulnerability, Mia whispered, as her tongue rounded the curves of his lobe, "Io volere tu dentro me," expressing her desire for Ty to come inside her. As his fingers twined through her hair, he firmly pulled her head 'til their eyes met parallel, and softly recited a mutual favorite, "I've Made Love to You a Thousand Times" in Italian, "Io fabbricato essire inamorato tu un mille tempo."

Mia was released from the guilt of wanting feelings that had long escaped her, as Ty's tongue traveled the length of her neck to the top of her scalp. She pleaded for him to go down, "Abbasare, per favore!" gasping in disbelief at the feeling of deep pleasure.

Ty licked her lips, "Non c'e'diprego," it's my pleasure, he said, gently laying her back, raising her skirt with his mouth, exposing her well-manicured Brazilian wax where he laid his tongue gently, firmly on her clit, rotating it around her soft, wet, palpitating bareness.

This drew immense moisture, seemingly from her whole being – from her imagination to every nerve ending in her limbs. Her body began to tense as he rose from between the tall redwood of her legs, throwing them over his chiseled shoulders and slowly thrusting himself into her. "Andare profondo per favore, librare ti in mi!" Mia began screaming for Ty to go deep, to release himself inside her. As the sweat dripped from his forehead onto her breast, Mia moaned in indecipherable, mutated English and Italian, "Si, si, si, gracie, thank you!" They climaxed simultaneously, a climax sealed with a deep, passionate kiss. The spontaneity and intimate indulgence of this night with Ty re-ignited a teenage-like fire and passion in Mia's soul.

An hour passed and they finally came to a stop where they had first started at the courthouse steps. Making love to Mia on the same streets that Bri controlled underscored the firm courage Ty kept tucked under his reserved demeanor. Mia and Ty walked from the carriage as if they were approaching the Green Mile and its long road of waiting despair. They sought to hold on to as much of the night as they could, embracing for a passionate kiss to end their defining, magical evening. The beginning of something the ending of which neither of them could fathom.

Mia hopped into her pearlescent convertible Mercedes 550 coupe with no thought of the time, which now approached 2 a.m., and no inclination to conjure up an alibi. She didn't carry an atom's weight of concern. She drifted in the residual bliss of making love to Ty, belting out Switch's "*A Dream*" as she drove. "*A dream….a simple fantasy that I wish was reality*"… then the phone rang.

"Where the hell you at?" Bri roared. "I don't know who you think you fucking with, I'm dealing with..." Mia hung up, numb to her husband's hateful disrespect. For tonight, she refused to break the rhythm of her song or leave the love high she still rode. From that night on, Mia's bold actions went largely ignored, because Bri was inundated by his own street indiscretions and infidelities.

I-69..70 to Lakeside

Finding time to spend with Ty became a welcome distraction. Mia's sense of spontaneity began to parallel Ty's, as she opened up to going and doing whatever, whenever, and wherever he took her. Before long she'd become acquainted with Ty's family, comfortable hanging around with them. Ty jokingly described his family as a cross between the Evans' family of "Good Times" and the Clampetts of "The Beverly Hillbillies," families bound by closeness, camaraderie and comical controversy. Mia loved it, as it was a bond she'd never seen before. Every weekend was some celebration or occasion, full of aunts, uncles, cousins, brothers and sisters. Equally enamored was Ty's family with Mia, and not just with her beauty.

Ty's family witnessed the chemistry between the two – a bliss that oozed from their public shows of affection, unending laughter and smiles, and their teenage demeanors around each other. Understanding Mia's marital status, the whole family was protective of their relationship; everyone worked to preserve this happiness, regardless of any societal moral or ethical concern.

Completely relaxed, comfortable and trusting for the first time since the loss of her father, Mia felt normalcy and love, as if Ty's arms were her natural habitat. Every weekend with Ty felt like celebrating a holiday. This weekend it actually was; it was Ty's birthday and he'd promised to celebrate with his cousins.

As with many times before, today found Mia and Ty inseparable, as she would accompany Ty and his cousins and brother on a "ride." It had become a tradition for Ty, his brothers and cousins to gather and caravan to the lake and camp out. His younger brother, Mit Ramal, was the connoisseur and purveyor of the marijuana leaf, always jokingly claiming glaucoma, rheumatoid or some other medical excuse for using his weed. With only enough room in the cab for three, Mia and Ty giddily chose to ride in the bed of the Ford Ranger truck. The weather was perfect, and they were cooled by the wind of the moving vehicle. Ty made it as comfortable as he could for Mia, laying out two comforters with a rolled camping bag as a pillow, so they could lounge. They experienced a rush from the open air and upward view of the clouds. Their spontaneity left them completely oblivious to the passing cars or the presence of the three inside of the cab watching them, and drew a rush that heightened their sexual adrenaline. Ty pulled Mia close, kissing her neck as he moved his hands in her pants, cupping her and running his fingers deep inside her. Without prompting she pulled down her jeans, exposing her black thongs with faux diamonds sparkling in the back. Ty raised her blouse, licking her banana-crème breasts and nipples that were as chocolate as Hershey kisses. The excitement was so intense that Mia had cum from the deep, gentle thrust of his fingers in her love well, and the soft caress of his lips and tongue on her breasts. Ty threw her legs into the open sky, resting them around the small of his toned back as he slid inside her, around her soaked thong. With intense emotion, they made love from the east stretches of the city, across Interstate 70 until they reached Creve Coeur Lake on the far northwestern edge of Maryland Heights. Mia's climax reached its pinnacle, lips palpitated endlessly as she lay numb in Ty's arms, unable to release her claw-like grip on his back. They shared a mutual glance of immense pleasure as they lay looking into what had now become night's ascent, the sun rendezvousing with the horizon over the lake.

At this moment, Mia began to assess the burgeoning depths of her feelings for Ty, and what it meant for her marriage and future with

Bri. For Mia, this relationship had transcended the thrill of cat and mouse, grown beyond the feeling of a temporary fix until she gained emotional footing in her current relationship. Thoughts of feeling his touch and hearing his words, soothing as a sonata to her ears, were nearly constant. She desired to mimic and topple the intensity of each spontaneous action with the next one. They shared an emotional co-dependency and thirst for one another. The sun signed off for the night and yielded its position to the full moon, as Ty interrupted Mia's moment of calm reflection.

"Mia, baby, I, I….," Ty hesitantly searched for the right words to express his love, but before he could, Mia released him from his hesitation with her own expression. "Ty, I love you. I never intended to, but I don't even question why anymore…," Mia said, as Ty stopped her with a kiss. "Baby, every moment we have is ours, I don't know about tomorrow, Bri, or anything else, but I know you've touched me," Ty said. "Well, I'll ride 'til the tank hits E!" Mia smiled as she wiped the trail of a tear from her face. They ended their lake trip as they started, in the flatbed of the truck, in each other's arms as if on a moving island. They both knew their pledge of love was the genesis of what would likely prove another long, hard, if not gratifying situation.

On another long, hard ride home, Mia pumped her fist through the dropped top of her 550, listening to Marvin Gaye's "You Sure Love to Ball." The song was one of Ty's favorites from a CD he had compiled for her. She felt a residual tingle from Ty's touch, and the moisture between her thighs had yet to dry. She could not hold in her intense feelings of ecstasy, especially in light of her personal turmoil, so she called her trusted confidante, Pam. Mia knew Pam would not judge her, nor take the joy from this moment.

Days passed, and Mia was met each morning since the lake by the text messages she and Ty sent to each other the previous night. The noon time usually meant the delivery of flowers to her desk from Ty, and the nights beckoned with another chance for them to meet. Mia's behavior might not be noted by some, but her spirited, upbeat demeanor in the midst of Bri's verbal and mental abuse irked him. Bri liked her off guard and unsettled so she couldn't think critically and zone in on his indiscretions. Bri began to notice tweaks in her everyday behavior. Mia had never been one to sleep with her phone, but she began keeping it as close as her pillow, going to the bathroom more often in the middle of the night. Mia was given to more journaling and spending more time on her consulting business at the computer. This gave her cover to maneuver her schedule and conversations without arousing suspicion, at even the most inopportune times of the night.

She'd never needed an excuse before, but now was different. She found herself in a game she had never played, against a player who seemed to master the board. Bri was limited in his own knowledge of computers or even mobile technologies, but running a business made it unavoidable. At 2 a.m., Bri sat in the lounge of their master bedroom for hours after a fight between him and Mia, collecting his thoughts.

CHAPTER XIV

Cheating in the Next Room

Between the tense arguments and fights, communication between Bri and Mia was relegated to sharply-worded verbal snares and cold, steely stares. From their lounge, Bri, who was only partially awake, noticed the light illuminating from her cell phone. He calmly walked into their master suite and asked, "what's up, what you doin'?" His eyes beamed large through the dark of the night, surprising Mia, who had just laid down the phone upon hearing his approach. She acted as if she had been awakened from her sleep. "Humm?" Mia murmured, in a scruffy-falsetto voice. "Wha, what's up?"

"Nothin', just seein' if you were OK!" Bri said, returning to their lounge. He knew she was lying, although she thought she'd covered well. She had no idea that he'd routed her outgoing texts and emails to his computer. Going through the list of emails, he saw one time-stamped 1:15 a.m., just before he'd questioned her. The email was sent to TP. It read: "You know I'll follow your lead wherever you go." Bri quickly gathered the TP stood for Tyson Penn, his supposed friend, Ty. Bri was keen at connecting the dots on people, so although this came as no surprise, he still found it troubling, to say the least, to know that in the lone wake of early morn, her thoughts were filled with someone else. But he kept cool, waiting out the night.

Morning couldn't arrive fast enough. Bri needed to address in his own way his dissatisfaction at what must be developing between Ty and Mia. The sun was rising as Bri jumped up liked a Muslim about to miss his morning prayer. He suited up and headed out to grab coffee, but not before greeting Mia in an uncharacteristically jovial manner.

"See you later, baby, I got some work to do!" he said, catching Mia off guard. This kind of action is what made Bri an unpredictable, hard read. "OK," she said, mildly perplexed.

Bri met his "handyman" at his morning spot, the coffee shop in the Loop. "What's up, Knuck?" Bri said. "Well, it's gotta be something, because I'm definitely not tryin' to be woke at six in the morning!" Knuck said with a grin.

"I just need you to deliver a message to my new friend. He's taken the dangerous liberty of a liaison with my wife," Bri instructed. His fierce demeanor was in stark contrast to the calm he'd exuded in the house, and what he would typically employ, especially in public. Bri was taken aback by the emotions that had arisen. Nothing else needed to be said. Knuck clearly understood who, when and how. Bri was aware that Mia planned to meet Ty later that evening for dinner, under the guise of a business meeting. Mia employed her own "don't ask, don't tell" policy, so if Bri didn't ask who, what or where, she didn't voluntarily tell. Ty was in route to their meeting spot at Liluma's restaurant as Mia headed out the door to meet him. "Hey, baby…" Bri said, stunning her out of the blue.

"Don't do that! You scared me!" Mia, already on pins and needles hoping that nothing would be found out, nearly shouted.

"Didn't want to scare you, I just wanted to surprise you. We've been movin' past each other like ships in a wide ocean. I wanna drop everything tonight and spend some time with my baby. So, I made reservations for us!" Bri smiled, with all the charm he could muster. "I know I've been neglecting you," he added, his words capped with a look of sincerity. Mia listened, dumbfounded by timing and bewildered by what could be at the root of his sentiments. She tried to think quickly, searching for a reaction that wasn't negative but still saved her night with Ty.

She didn't want to turn down this uncommon nicety, but hated being forced to choose between her man and her "strange," as the older generation might call Ty. Momentarily silent, Mia pondered Bri's overture as he kissed her and simultaneously placed a pearl necklace around her neck, grabbed her hand and led her out the door. "Oh, and tonight, let's leave our phones behind," Bri suggested nonchalantly, hoping she'd believe he simply wanted them to focus solely on one another.

Mia had been so stunned by Bri's stealth approach, that she couldn't manufacture anything but a smile, and a subtle, "OK!" She didn't know, of course, that he carried an extra phone for conducting his own personal affairs, but he had successfully managed to cut off her communication with Ty for the evening; Ty, who still expected her to show up at Liluma's. As Mia sat quietly in the front seat, Prince's "*Scandalous*" was muted by her thoughts of Ty. She still didn't give much thought to the possibility that Bri might have been on to something.

Smiling Faces Sometimes tell Lies..

Bri's smile, wide across his face, pronounced not his joy at spending time with Mia, but his confidence over what he knew was the imminent fate of Ty Penn. He could just as easily have allowed his wife's rendezvous to take place so that Mia could've seen the damage first-hand, or even have Mia touched as well. But Bri was more calculating than that, enjoying the thrill of making her wonder. He felt certain Mia would not connect the dots, which jazzed him even more, giving him a firm sense of mental superiority.

This part of the game sat at the root of a hustler's mentality – manipulation and the estimation of a person's reach, understanding, predicting their movements like re-runs of a movie scene.

As Bri drove Mia to their dinner out, Ty traveled westbound on Delmar toward Euclid, stopping for the light at Taylor. West of Grand, the crime rate was considerably higher above the city's average. He drove in his usual musically-induced driving stupor, his surroundings drowned out by a perfect mix of treble and bass coming from his speakers. He sang along to Anthony Hamilton's *"Do You Feel Me"* as his thoughts raced forward to meeting Mia in just moments. Coming up on his right, a 1981 Buick Regal pulled just shy of his blind spot, and as he glimpsed in the rearview mirror… "tat tat tat tat…tat!" Shots rang out like fireworks from a rust-laden '77 Caprice Classic with tinted windows, immediately parallel to his driver's side door. The next few seconds seemed like an eternity as Ty sped up, swerving away from the car, jumping the curb and rolling over onto a grassy vacant knoll less than a mile away from where he was to meet Mia. As Ty lay unconscious and bloodied in his upside-down vehicle, Mia sat eerily with Bri in the same place she and Ty had planned to meet for dinner. Throughout dinner, Mia mustered smiles and tried to stay distracted from her worry of Ty. She tried her best to enjoy the pleasure of Bri's company. But the smiles began to weigh on Mia's facial muscles, settling into an intense headache. The minutes passed like hours, and she became intoxicated by the thought of the unknown.

Bri's warm words of affection couldn't reach her – she felt numb, deafened to anything outside her own head. Bri didn't really care; he knew the root of her discomfort and having this edge gave him extreme pleasure. Ty being gone satisfied his insatiable desire for revenge; unfortunately, it would leave him without influence within certain political bureaucracies Ty navigated so easily.

"Hey baby, you enjoy that tilapia?" Bri asked.

Mia sat motionless, flashing an empty smile. "Yeah, it's great. I'm just feeling a little woozy. I think I need to just go home and lay it down!" she told him apologetically.

"OK, honey, whatever you need. Let's go," Bri responded in a gentlemanly manner, pulling her chair out.

"Thanks," she said, suddenly realizing that none of this made sense. Baby...honey, dinner, chairs? The timing was too coincidental. Although she'd longed for this kind of attention and kindness, it was no longer welcomed from Bri, not at this stage in their relationship. She craved it only from Ty. Even so, she refused to accept that Ty's continued presence was furthering the alienation between her and Bri. She couldn't appreciate it from Bri because his abuse had closed a door permanently between them. She'd opened a door to the room of the forbidden; shredding to pieces the Pandora's Box in the process. At home, Mia tried not to be too conspicuous rushing to her phone. Bri wandered about the lower levels of the manse or wound down in the lounge of their master suite, allowing her the space to exchange her secret texts and emails. But tonight was different. Bri climbed into bed when Mia did and cuddled up next to her. Mia lay there, confused, questioning the road she'd traveled, rolling away and rejecting what she'd so often said she desired from her husband. Her heart seemed sealed by her desires for another man.

"God, I feel like I'm cheating on my guy with my husband." Mia was thrown into a moral and emotional conundrum. There would be no communication with Ty at least until the morning.

Mia watched every minute pass on the clock 'til the sun rose, finally jumping from the bed like a soldier being called to quarters. When she couldn't reach Ty at home or on his cell, Mia reached out to his secretary, Ingrid. "Yes, Ingrid? Has Ty come into the office yet?" she asked.

"Oh, Mia!" Ingrid's voice was almost panicky.

"Oh, Mia, what?" Mia anxiously asked.

"Something happened. Matter of fact, turn on the news right now!" As the news report came on… "Last night, a well-known attorney was critically injured near the Central West End in what appears to have been a drive-by shooting. Attorney Tyson Penn was rushed to Barnes-Jewish Hospital shortly after midnight, where he remains in critical condition. We'll keep you updated on any new developments," the news anchor said somberly, as pictures of Ty's car and the ambulance flashed eerily across the screen. Mia did her best not to react, even as panic filled her. Bri lounged in bed, listening to the same report with glee, feigning concern for his business contact and swallowing the satisfaction over his feat.

Mia threw on clothes and rushed out of the house, mumbling an excuse to Bri, who told her he was still "wore out" from the night before. She raced to the hospital, but was turned away before she could get to his room.

"I'm here to see Tyson Penn," Mia told the guard. He flipped through his clipboard. "Ma'am, I'm sorry, your name is not on the blackout list."

A week passed and Mia could not get a single update on his condition. She wandered through the week like a zombie, unable to focus on anything at work, every moment filled with dread at the thought of Ty being gone, never hearing his voice again. On the eighth day, her desk phone rang. With the enthusiasm of a meth addict on the first day of rehab, she answered, "Hello, this is Mia. How may I help you?"

"Whoa – who died?" a scratchy voice asked.

"Excuse me, sir, how may I help you?" Mia had little patience and was too exhausted to mask it.

"Well, you can start by bringing me some mangoes and a maybe a good book?" the voice said.

"Ty! Oh my God, Tyson?!" she exclaimed, as her eyes welled with tears. His weak voice was almost unrecognizable, 'til he mentioned mangoes. Ty had introduced Mia to the mango, especially its effect on the female libido.

"Damn, girl. You didn't write my obituary already, did ya? Yeah, it's me!" he said. Tears flowed as she raced from her office straight to the hospital. Reports had hit the paper and TV about the upgrade of Ty's condition from critical to fair and his expected release. Word got quickly back to Bri, whose anger swelled. And he had no doubt that Mia would run to Ty's side, full of sympathy and love.

After the attempt on his life, Ty, at the behest of Mia, decided to lay low, hoping information would surface about who was behind the failed hit. In the far reaches of both their minds floated the possibility that Bri was the culprit.

Ty was not one to have enemies. He combed his memories, trying to recall a statement that Bri had made in jest about Mia having greater accessibility to Ty than himself. Bri's comments had been mixed with laughter, and although Ty had let the statements go, he felt a needling worry that seeds had taken root in Bri's mind about something more. Although Bri accepted Ty as Mia's legal counsel, they both accepted that Ty was his primary business connect. Mia was the front for most of Bri's business and financial transactions because he had legal hurdles yet to cross, not to mention hefty government fines that had been levied against him by the courts as part of his previous sentence plea. This, of course, made Ty's direct relationship with Mia all the more justified.

Mia also considered the possibility of Bri's involvement in the attempt on Ty's after recalling how Bri had shoved her, taunting her with the question, "Who you gonna call? Your *legal* counsel?!" the emphasis on "legal" underscoring his doubts about the true nature of her relationship with Ty.

Nevertheless, although nothing had been said overtly, it was clear that tension existed between the two. Even if the roots of the tension were unripe and unsubstantiated, Bri's pedigree came from the streets, and he hadn't climbed the hustler food chain by being naïve. He remained chummy and continued to extend respectful courtesies to Ty when they met. Still, he instructed Knuck to keep a watchful eye on Ty. Bri was never one to show emotion, viewing everyone as pawns in his game, so there was no need to change his strategy.

He attended to the business at hand and he needed both Mia and Ty to do so, but he knew every man had a breaking point. Ty, still laid low by his injuries, had been absent for nearly two months. This had taken a tremendous emotional toll on both Mia and himself. She wondered if Ty would make an appearance at her upcoming 40th birthday party, surprising her as he had done on many occasions.

CHAPTER XV

Cold War

Thursday night at Movado featured a packed house of the St. Louis's social elite. Although 40 was the pinnacle of social birthday celebrations, Mia's smile was one of only obligation. Without Ty, the night was no different than any other, and her anticipation waned as the night passed. She leaned her head back on her seat, glancing at the door every time it opened. Ty, dressed in an Armani blazer and shirt she'd given him, finally walked through the door. Seeing him, Mia beamed, her dutiful smile finally real. He embraced her boldly, discreetly whispering, "Io amare tu!" expressing his love for her in Italian. His presence and words re-ignited her fire.

Ever attentive to the man-code of respect, however, Ty immediately sought out Bri to extend his respects and show his "love," congratulating him on a successful night. Bri greeted Ty, escorting him to the club office. "It's you, baby, you made this happen!" Bri told him, as all of Ty's legal work on his behalf along the way made his lifestyle possible. But Bri's puffery fell on deaf ears – no flattery, no money mattered to Ty…his focus was on Mia.

Throughout the night, Ty and Mia stole glances over the crowds. The thrill of their secret created a chemistry that was nearly combustible. Ty finally approached her, breaking the laborious eye play, and boldly asked her to the floor midway through a song. He gestured to Bri for his approval before engaging. Bri watched uncomfortably before abruptly nodding his approval. He stayed cool, but felt that Ty was fast approaching out of bounds in a way that he could only take as disrespect. Mia's body begged to draw close, but she knew all eyes were glued on the dance floor, so she remained conservative in her embrace. "What are we doing, Ty?" Mia whispered softly through her teeth.

"I'm dancing with a queen...and I got permission from the king!" Ty said, smiling sarcastically. Ty used all of his inner strength not to pull her close and press his lips to hers. His good sense seemed to erode with every note of the song, their pretense spared only by its ending.

Moving from the dance floor through the packed crowd, Mia felt his hardness pressed against her. She purred her deep wanting, thinking "Damn, I want that," as she teasingly pressed into him. As Mia took her seat past Bri, he glanced at her with disgust and contempt.

VIP privileges had always been extended to Ty, even at times clearing out the space to accommodate him and any unexpected guests he might bring along. This time, though, as Ty approached the section, Bri signaled to his security to restrict him access to the section. "It's full!" Knuck said, waving Ty off. Ty understood, but glanced around, appearing puzzled, at the obviously empty seats. Keeping his composure, he shot Mia a cool smile and wink, then walked toward the DJ booth. Mia could feel the tension, not knowing what to expect because Bri's office was stationed behind the DJ's booth. She felt powerless even as her inclination was to safeguard Ty, especially after the previous attempt on his life. Knuck worked his way in the same direction like a slow-moving

Mack truck. This was a sign that their Cold War had begun – heightened tensions, calculated moves, but nothing drastic enough for outsiders to notice. Ty stopped at the DJ booth, slipping the DJ a twenty. He decided to speak to Mia in a mode he knew she'd understand. He requested the GAP Band's "No Hiding Place". The lyrics clearly conveyed his desires. Her back was to Ty, but their eyes met in the mirror. She flashed a smile, biting her lip, affirming that she'd gotten the message and that she thoroughly approved. Bri got the message as well. He stormed away from the VIP area, infuriated by their cat and mouse theatrics. As Ty left the club not long after the song, he waved one last birthday greeting and was gone. Mia's night, at least the happy part of her birthday, came to a screeching halt, and she covered her disappointment with her obligatory smile of propriety for her guests. After a brief taste of Ty's presence, Mia was left to starve for his smile, his touch, his tongue. When she turned back from the exit door, her eyes met Bri's furious stare, slowly nodding up and down, and finally left to right in dismay. Mia failed to engage his stare or what it might mean, still lost in the bliss of Ty's presence. She was becoming carelessly wayward, telling of one not accustomed to the game. As the night finally wound down, only a few hours had passed since Ty left the club, and Bri was still filled with a fiery rage.

"We closin' up! Everybody out! We'll cover down and close out tomorrow!" Bri said, dismissing the wait staff and clean-up crews. Mia knew Bri's boiling points all too well and she saw it register off the scale now. Mia counted the money from the door while Bri locked the last of the doors letting the remaining staff out. Mia intentionally focused her attention away from Bri. His frustration was heightened by the fact that Mia acted as if nothing unusual had happened throughout the night. Mia's demeanor was typically a rational counter to Bri's normally calm self. His calm had always allowed him to control their conversations. He was accustomed to getting an aimless or misdirected emotional response to his taunts. Mia had always been easily frustrated by Bri's indifference to her inability to convey the root of her emotion, but now it was Bri who seethed with a misguided, aimless anger, heightened by Mia's apparent indifference. "So, you ain't got nothin' to say?" He bit his lip, staring Mia down as her eyes stayed fixed on counting the money.

"Well, it was a good night!" Mia answered with sarcastic enthusiasm.

"I'm sure it was QUEEN!" Bri yelled in anger, mocking Ty's reference to her from the dance floor.

"What's up, Bri? It's my birthday, can I at least enjoy the last hour of my day?" she sassed.

"What's up? What's UP?!" Bri fumed, knocking the lockbox out of her hands. Grabbing her by the neck, "Trick, who the hell you think you playin' with?" his voice seethed with rage, his eyes reddened by anger, Hennessy and cocaine.

"What? Trick? You the one on some trick mess!" Mia said, shoving him off. "Maybe that's your own conscience from bangin' these flea bags around the whole damn city, and even in the club…the club, Brandon, OUR damn club!" she continued. "Oh yeah, you don't think I know. Dude, Ray Charles could see the game you on!" she added.

"You have lost your damn mind!" Bri said, turning away with a smirk that would've affirmed Mia's claims. "You didn't answer my damn question. What's up with Ty?" Bri asked again.

"You got the audacity to ask me what's up; maybe I should be bangin' him right in VIP!" Mia spit at him, and the words inspired a backhand that drove her onto the floor. They'd both entered the dark world of infidelity, enjoying forbidden pleasures that had cast them into the murky shadows of remorse and an abyss of lurking dangers. For Mia, the dangers were more present and volatile. In Bri's mind, the mere thought of her stepping out was just as bad as the physical intimacy itself.

They'd already bypassed any possible degree of forgiveness, understanding or acceptance. The dark recesses of Bri's mind had already been breached – his beastly thoughts of revenge were fueled by a polarizing anger when he wondered what is, had been and could be between his wife and his friend. As she sat on the floor with her head in her hands, Mia came to her senses, trading silence for safety. "Alright, Bri...OK," Mia whispered submissively, reaching out for calm.

Inside, though, Mia burned with a resolve, knowing this moment was the road sign for her imminent exit. She picked herself up, as Bri walked away, unremorseful. She left the club quietly, not bothering with the money he'd strewn across the floor. Nothing mattered more to her than getting out. Riding home, she looked in the mirror, watching her eye begin to swell. She smiled when the Whisper's "Lost and Turned Out" came on the radio, understanding that this was her message, this was her "Freedom Train." She raced home to pack her things before Bri returned, and hurriedly left for her mother's. Packed with only essentials and what few outfits fit into her travel bag, Mia knocked on her mother's door. "Hey, Ma!"

Mia started, and began to cry. Savita needed no words; her daughter's swollen face told her all she needed to know. She opened her arms and Mia stumbled into them shaking. "Come on in, my baby, it's gonna be all right!"

Two months had passed since Mia left Bri for the safety of her mother's house. The sexually explicit text and voice messages she'd retrieved from Bri's phone, the eyewitness accounts of his sexual trysts and the continued verbal abuse finally compelled Mia to accept Ty's old offer of a small getaway. He refused to specify where, only to add to the intrigue. Warmed by the mere thought of spending some quality time with Ty, Mia decided to give him a call; wondering whether his offer was even still there. The phone rang three times before Ty picked up. He knew it was Mia from the caller ID; this was his subtle way of drawing upon her sense of anticipation. "Hello?" Ty answered.

"Heyyy, stranger!" Mia said, her voice laced with sensuous longing.

"Who is dis?" Ty questioned jokingly.

"What! It's me, boy...Mia - stop playing!" she said.

"Girl, I'm kidding, you know I'd know your voice with a deaf man's ears!" Ty grinned, drawing a chuckle from the other end of the phone.

"So, are my reservations still valid?" Mia asked, hoping he'd remember his previous invitation to take her away.

"Well, you might have to come over and put a deposit down now!" Ty teased. Not long ago, Mia had been torn between putting maximum effort into salvaging her marriage with Bri, or figuring

131

out how to build a new relationship with whom she believed to be her truer love, Ty. Her marriage had been challenged from the cutting of the cake, though, and since Mia considered forty an age of re-birth and renewal, her perspective had changed. Her emotional fuse had shortened, and a desire for self-fulfillment had become her priority. Mia was once inclined to honor social and moral propriety, but now she decided she'd no longer be a prisoner to social dictates and ethical referendums if they meant staying trapped in an abusive marriage. Her desire to give and receive freely moved her to risk her soul to heal and satisfy her heart.

 It would, if nothing else, lift her from the abyss of loneliness, depression and agitation, and allow her to climb to a plateau of passion and ecstasy with Ty. Wherever his invitation led her, she'd submit without hesitation. She imagined this as her Stella moment, and looked forward to getting her groove back. After getting off the phone with Ty, she immediately called Pam, who was uniquely positioned in Mia's relationship with Bri, as she held the trust and confidence of them both. Unfortunately, Mia had no idea how deep the confidence between Bri and Pam had grown, and she confided everything to Pam.

A Night to Forget…The Connection

For Bri, Pam was just a pawn, a way to stay securely aware of Mia's thoughts and movements. For Pam, her own internal conflict weighed on the core of her decency and her friendship. She had long been drawn to Mia for her beauty and the cheery disposition that had led her to being voted Most Popular their senior year in high school. As she began her excited rant about her getaway with Ty, Pam reflected back to one night during their senior year. Mia had just broken up with her boyfriend and was in a fragile, vulnerable state. In tears and nearly frantic with rage, Mia drove to Pam's apartment two nights before homecoming. Pam's social indulgences were already well beyond her years. She was known to drink and smoke weed, and her sexual exploits, whether true or rumored, were a school legend. Matter of fact, Pam rarely dated her age contemporaries, preferring older men of means and status. Pam tried to listen attentively, through a haze of Alize and weed smoke, to Mia lamenting her break-up. Sensing the extent of her friend's vulnerability, Pam removed Mia's shoes and started a friendly massage of her head and temples, seeking to help Mia relax.

She convinced Mia to try a little Wild Irish Rose, and quietly dropped some X into her drink. Mia liked the sweetness of the Rose, and the euphoric effects of the ecstasy came over her slowly. This stealth combination threw Mia into a semi-conscious, drug-induced stupor. Pam had already convinced Mia to change into some spare night clothes and stay for a girls' night. She slipped Mia's borrowed silk pajamas off. "Wha, wha, wait, waasa, you…" Mia murmured, in an incoherent slur. She gave up and as her eyes began to roll and her resistance waned. As Mia's eyes shuttered, Pam gently opened her shirt and found Mia's breast with her tongue. Touch was Mia's only working sense at the moment, and she could not decipher the gender of the fingers working their way inside her, nor indentify the tongue that produced the sobering orgasm. The night had passed, and Pam awakened to a look of dismay and confusion on Mia's face as she lay struggling to piece together the night before. Pam feigned ignorance, blaming the alcohol. "What happened, I was totally out of it?" she mumbled, as Mia slowly shook her head and lowered her eyes, leaving unspoken a secret she hoped never to speak. Pam, however, reveled in the memory of the night, knowing she'd had a taste of something for which many men had wished and schemed. The memory now sped through Pam's head as she held the phone, listening to Mia. She snapped back into the conversation, interrupting Mia, who had been talking non-stop. "What about Bri, girl?" Pam abruptly interjected.

"What about Bri?" Mia snapped back. She was taken off guard by the question, because Pam had never concerned herself with Bri's interests before. "Oh, don't get a righteous conscience now!" Mia scolded. "Pam, you know where I'm at and you know what I've been through. I thought at least my ace would be excited for me!" she sighed.

"Girl, I'm just sayin'...I guess you gotta do you!" Pam replied enviously. In Pam's mind, Mia had it all – a model's figure with cover girl beauty, popularity and one of the most successful hustlers on the streets. They lived in a beautiful home, she was a successful professional in her own right, and now, had her own tender side piece in Ty. Not to mention the seven carat, Cartier diamond that adorned her left ring finger. For Mia, the trappings of materialism were no more than empty calories. And although Pam still fancied herself Mia's ace, envy had burned hidden inside her for years; it was this envy that fueled Pam's pursuits behind Mia's back. Pam was the originator of many of the rumors that resulted in the fights in which Mia often found herself center ring. It was Pam who introduced Mia to Bri, and Mia had never questioned the origin of their relationship. She knew Pam was the daughter of Big Red Wright and that he'd been one of the last of a dying breed of notorious ghetto kingpins, and she'd heard Bri mention that Red was the grandson of the well-respected and powerful Stagger Lee, whose exploits had been immortalized in folklore and song. Big Red had given Bri his start in the game, providing him finance, protection and counsel. He mentored Bri from the time Bri got out of juvie, as he'd done with other boys coming out of the detention center. Not to impart moral responsibility, of course, but to breed whatever street talents for which they showed promise.

Pam was 10 years Bri's junior when Big Red took him under his wing. She was only 16, but she'd developed the body of a woman. Bri, who was a mainstay in their home, manipulated her teen crush, introducing Pam to getting high and ultimately coaxing her into having sex with him. At one point he even got her pregnant then forced her, against her will, to abort. Bri knew that if Big Red ever found out, he'd have him killed or at least tortured, on a good day. This history of secrets bonded Bri and Pam, forever emotionally linking them. Mia knew nothing of any of it, and Pam always wondered how it would all ultimately play out. Big Red was out of the way for now, serving twenty-five to thirty on a conspiracy charge at the Potosi Correctional Facility. Pam was doing her best to honor her trusted friend, continually struggling to subvert her own feelings for Bri and the uncontrollable attraction and envy she'd long harbored for Mia. Even with Pam's lukewarm reception to her plans with Ty, Mia's excitement grew with the thought of their secret excursion. She knew leaving behind the stress of finding the time and space to alone would only heighten their intimate connection. Every day since meeting him at the steps of Kiener Plaza, she'd fantasized of being on an island with one who owned her heart, mind, body and every inch of her loving soul. She quickly gathered herself to run across town to Ty's. Cruising through the downtown traffic, she hummed to a mix tape Ty'd made for her, the Whisper's "Olivia" setting the rhythm.   Not a slow song played that didn't speak to an emotion she harbored for Ty. She arrived at his place at quarter past seven.

Visit to Ty's Loft

His loft opened to a unique, spacious view of the downtown skyline. The living room was positioned perfectly to capture daily views of both the rising and setting of the sun. Since that first date, watching the setting of the sun had become a treasured ritual they shared. Their night rendezvous were always timed for such. As Ty opened the door, she flung herself helplessly into his open arms, her smile stretching almost as wide. She growled low, tongue in teeth, blowing her warm breath into his ear. "Heyyy Ty-ger, I'm your prey," she whispered, then opened her full length coat to expose her tasteful nakedness, wearing nothing but the red stilettos she knew he adored. As Maxwell's "Till the Cops Come Knocking," sang through his surround system; they sat on the chaise, whetting their palates, with a medley of blackberries and Camembert cheese, and glasses of 1968 Chateau de Montaigne, the very wine they'd sipped the first time they made love in the carriage. Ty, ever the voyeur, laid Mia back upon the chaise and spread the expanse of her legs within clear view of the windows that ran the stretch of his wall. "So you think you got that sunshine? I'm gonna let the sun set over this horizon!" Ty teased.

Mia moaned incoherently as he laid just a tip of himself inside her, slowly inching deeper with every moment of the sun's descent. By the time the night had been fully ushered in, Ty finally quieted Mia's desperate pleas of want, now fully inside her, scaling every corner of her walls. "Baby, is this enough down payment?" Mia cooed.

"Nah, change of policy, no layaway…back it all up!" Ty forcefully commanded, firmly grasping Mia's hair. Not to be outdone by the physicality of her stallion, Mia rode her rush of adrenaline, bringing

137

her hips up to meet his thrust. Reversing the sexual momentum, she backed him into the wall, riding him like Roy Rogers rode Trigger, until he wailed, "Daaaaaamn!"

CHAPTER XVI

Growing Suspicions

Bri had grown increasingly suspicious of Mia's relationship with Ty over the few weeks they'd been separated. Bri knew he had all but relinquished his right to question Mia, and even those close to Bri noticed Mia's transformation and the unfamiliar joyous glow radiating from her very soul.

Bri had always believed himself to be the sole object of her happiness because he mistakenly equated his ability to meet her material wants with having an unshakeable hold on her.

Away from him, Mia was defining for herself the value of peace and love, and having tasted the likes of being loved as deeply as Ty loved her, she recognized more clearly the artificial roots of materialism. Her life had shifted into a dynamic new love paradigm. Even in Ty's absence, she felt a residual bliss that reverberated in her core. With each passing day, the mountainous reign Bri had long held over Mia's heart, seemed more distant. He'd been dethroned, his iron rule over her life crumbling into ruin and nothingness. She felt free.

This freedom was not so kind to Bri, however. He found himself forced to come to grips with a feeling foreign to him… he needed Mia. He'd never acknowledged a feeling of dependency on anyone in his life, but he found himself needing her. Not only for the part she played in his daily scheming, but for his hidden dream, an unspoken dream of settling down and giving birth to the next generation. Bri had no idea what to do with this feeling, and that pissed him off. He'd rather see Mia without anyone if it wasn't him, even if that meant her life had to end. But he had to know, with utter certainty, that she was gone to him before he compassed his next move. So Bri turned to Pam, his unseen hand. He knew Pam would do anything to prove she was a bottom bitch, one who would be down for anything. A secret Bonnie to his clandestine Clyde. He'd always been able to keep tabs on Mia through her, and he immediately began working her for everything she knew. Bri dangled the carrot that she'd be number one in front of her, a carrot he dangled from his pants. Mia's separation from Bri was all the justification Pam needed to follow his lead. He called her, feigning despondency and the need for a friend.

Pam picked up the phone, surprised to see his number. "What's up, Pimpin'?" she asked, her joking nickname for him.

"Nobody understands what it takes to keep this thing together," Bri complained, hoping to engage Pam's sympathies.

"Look, man, I know it's hard, but you ain't never by yourself!" Pam's tone softened and Bri knew then he'd hooked her.

"No disrespect, but between you an' me, I've always wondered what it'd be like with you by my side. Damn, I could probably fly!"

Bri's words spun around Pam's thoughts like a spider web. "No disrespect taken…and I would have you flying like Apollo pimping!" Pam confidently affirmed.

"Ah ite, hot girl…look, I'm not too far from you, imma stop through to drop off a little sum'n." He arrived at Pam's shortly thereafter, and she opened the door, casually dressed in a t-shirt and low-rise, loose shorts with a glass of Hennessy in hand. Before Bri could speak, she quickly signaled him to be quiet motioning that Mia was on the phone in her other hand.

"So what's up girl, what's good?" Mia asked her.

"Girl, I think I messed around and caught the flu, I'm gonna rest and call you later," Pam said, sensing Mia might want to stop by. She faked a cough to drive home the lie.

Knowing Pam's weakness…money and powder, Bri sat on the sofa and spread a stack of $100 bills across the table with a bag of cocaine. Signaling Pam to the couch, "You wanna fly? Then let this be our moment!" Kissing Pam's hand, he placed his mouth around her middle finger.

"Let's fly!" she said. Pushing her shoulders so that she'd kneel, Bri dropped his pants and laced his longing with the first line of blow. She went down as quickly as the Dow Jones average during the Great Depression, sniffing the line and engaging the length of his loin. Two more lines would follow then Bri placed a hit of powder on his tip, turned Pam over the table, and drove her like Tiger on the 18th hole.

The blow numbed Bri's sensation and left a vibrating tingle on her clitoris that would last half an hour after she climaxed. Pam felt close to Bri that she had no trouble detaching her loyalty from Mia. She opened up beyond Bri's expectations. Bri back-doored his interest in Mia and inquired about Ty, instead. "So, what's up with your boy, Ty?" Bri asked Pam. "Huh - you should ask your girl, she all on 'at. I didn't want to tell you," she sighed.

"Yeahhh, it's cool. I've moved on, I got the world to conquer…I need someone who gonna ride for real," he said, without an apparent care in the world. He smiled and winked at Pam, "You figga dig me, baby!" Bri coasted.

"I got you, Pimpin'!" she said, like a dutiful soldier. Without prompting she added, "They're takin' a little getaway soon." This tidbit of information burned a fiery angst in Bri's chest, but he held his composure. It was important to keep Pam dangling on her string of delusional hope. "Maybe we need a getaway - you'd like that, huh?" Bri asked.

"Hell, yeahhh, let's make it happ'n, Cap'n!" Pam exclaimed enthusiastically.

"Ah ite, we'll see whatit do!" Bri answered, as they parted ways. He left her apartment hurriedly in a foul mood, speeding away as his Aston Martin Rapide blasted Lil Wayne's *"Hustla Musiq."* Any compassion left buried inside his dark interior had been decimated. Bri controlled every situation by never allowing himself full attachment. He reminded himself that although Mia had long been a pawn in his game, no matter how valuable she'd become, she remained expendable. Now, even more so. His hold and sway was irrevocably challenged as he wondered how he could extract the rest of the milk from this cow. He moved on emotional auto-pilot, and Ty's utility also took a backseat to Bri's seething need to exact revenge.

First he'd have to release himself from the quarter of a million dollar debt to Ty, money Ty had secured from investors to put into the club. One of Ty's recent attempts to distance himself from Bri's friendship was to call the loan due. *Why the hell would I pay a cat who served me for my woman*?" Bri thought to himself, growing more resolute in his angst, more committed to fix Ty. Yet he was cautious not to plan from straight emotion, knowing that was too great a risk. Ty, although not cut from the same street cloth as Bri, was a formidable foe with many connections, the kind that could easily cut without detection. So he focused for the moment on Mia, whose expendability was made even more delectable by the one million dollar life insurance policy Bri believed he held on Mia. In the fog of early marital bliss, Mia had signed the policy, believing that they'd hold policies together. Being wise to the underbelly of the streets, Bri knew that no drastic moves could be made on the heels of a break-up. An affair would automatically make that subject motive and suspect. He knew he had to reverse the situation, creating a plot that would bring Mia back closer. Ultimately, Ty would have to suffer some tragic accident and be labeled the scorned outside love interest. These plans would consume Bri. Without details of Mia's departure or return, he knew that clock was ticking. His pride would have to take a hit as he would now have to uncharacteristically give chase. Sitting motionless in his car, feeling his personal and financial worlds imploding, he dulled the anxiety with a cocktail of Oxycotin, Xanax and a shot of Bellevedere. This medically-induced cool enabled him to initiate contact with Mia. Picking up his cell phone, he dialed Mia's number with a deep sigh.

"Hello?" To his surprise, Mia answered on the last ring.

Caught In the Matrix

"Heyyy, how ya doing, Sunflower?" Bri used the pet name he'd given her in happier days, for her obsession with sunflower seeds. His voice stuttered with an awkward mix of apprehension and cool.

"Dude, wassup?" Mia's asked, curiosity giving way to mild hostility then aggravation.

"Listen, baby…" Bri began.

"Baby?" Mia stopped him short.

"OK, damn…Mia Farone-Whitmore!" Bri retorted. "OK, I get it. I don't want to cause you any more frustration or pain…" Bri said, pausing to gain her sympathy. "But it's real important I see you…I promise I'll be brief and then leave you be. Please!"

Bri pleading was out of character. With a long pause she put her trepidation aside and thought to herself, "Maybe this would bring some closure." His plea moved Mia to accommodate his request. "Look, I have a lot of errands to do, so I can only spare about forty-five minutes," she told him.

Game on. And game time was when Bri always seemed to shine. Hoping for a little nostalgia, he wore a dash of Issimiyake, her favorite cologne. He slid his feet into the eel-skin Ferragamo loafers she'd given him for their first anniversary. Most notable was his wedding band still shining on his finger. When he arrived on Mia's doorstep, her arms were full of boxes heading for the trash bin. "Hey, let me grab that for you," Bri gallantly lifted the load from her arms.

"Thank you," Mia said, flashing a quick smile. Inside, Bri was gentlemanly and warm, complimenting Mia on how beautiful she looked. His attention for her at the moment was real, although the game was still the game. His eyes slid over Mia's voluptuous curves, the sweat from her chores pulled the t-shirt snug over her skin, exposing her nipples ever-so-slightly. Bri thought, "*I gotta get one more taste!*"

Knowing Mia was watching him, he poignantly picked up a photo that lay packed in an open box. The picture was of them cutting their wedding cake. "I always wondered whether true happiness really leaves or does it just lay suspended, waiting to be re-awakened?" Bri said, as if to himself, in an orchestrated moment of tenderness just for Mia. The poetic expression relaxed her; she didn't know Bri had copped it from the popular radio of WGNU's "*Off the Record with TD and the Boss.*"

Bri recalled stories of his mother and father, their deaths, struggles and their impact in shaping his person. His tough core would not normally let him express this, but he had to play the game. "You know, I always wanted to have what time didn't afford my parents… a lasting happiness!" Bri began, working himself to tears in a scene that would beat Denzel out of an Oscar. "Mia, I just wanna say I'm sorry. I'd give up everything in the world if it could ease the hurt I've caused you," he added. Mia saw sincerity and humility, a façade fueled by the Oxy and Xanax, mixed with a little high-level jive. Mia capitulated. Her need to comfort bubbled to the surface, and as Bri's tears streamed, she held him, whispering within inches of his ear. "It's OK, it's OK, Bri, everything will work as it should," Mia assured her estranged husband, an apparently broken man. Believing his pain, Mia cupped his face in her hands, wiped his tears and kissed his forehead. He slowly raised his head until his eyes and lips were parallel with hers. The scent of his cologne, one of her favorites, stoked her pheromones.

With their bodies still touching from the fleeting moment of innocent comfort, their lips followed and Bri closed the remaining distance. In seconds, Mia found herself consumed by his subtle orchestrated emotional letting, now entangled in a deep, forbidden lip lock. Bri rushed her pants down over her hips like a high school jock in a locker room quickie. Mia lay motionless for the briefest moment, then and quickly shoved Bri away, thinking of Ty. Feelings of guilt, shame and betrayal overcame her, the impact sobering her. "You have to go! This should not have happened!" Mia exclaimed, nervously scrambling to compose herself. Bri beamed inside, pleased with how successfully he'd penetrated her emotional defenses, not bothered by the fact that his sexual feat lasted less than two minutes. In a larger sense, he felt a degree of vindication for this revenge on Ty.

"Mia, thanks for..."Bri started.

"Just please leave!" Mia demanded, unable to meet his eyes. As the door closed behind him, she slumped with her head in her hands. As moment passed, she felt complete affirmation that any emotional, mental and physical connection to Bri was dead and her feelings for Ty were real and exclusive. Guilt penetrated her core as she yearned to hear Ty's voice and feel his presence.

Ty's Return

As Ty returned from a speaking engagement at his alma mater, Boston University, the universe intervened. He phoned Mia in the midst of her emotional wrangling. She hesitated, but with a burst of elation she answered his call, immediately belting out a tune from Gerald Albright's *"You Don't Even Know… Such a captivating style and the sweetness of your smile, told me there's no resisting you…"*

"Damn, what's up baby, you miss me?" Ty laughed, stopping her in the midst of her tune.

"Yes, terribly! Baby, I need to see you!" she exclaimed. No matter what her request, he accommodated her. That's what attracted her to him.

"Nothing would please me more, baby!" Ty said. Ty rescheduled a meeting he'd previously set for his return to oblige Mia's request. Only minutes from the airport, Ty turned his modest Tesla onto her block. An environmentalist of sorts who believed in reducing his carbon footprint, Ty loved his electric car. To Mia, his social, political and environmental consciousness was sexy. Pulling up in front of the house, Ty was greeted by Mia running to his car and playfully jumping on it, sliding off to greet him. Tears streamed down her cheeks; embracing him as if he'd just returned from never.

With her head glued to his chest, "Baby, I really love you…more than I can express." Mia murmured urgently. Her intense spontaneity moved him, but puzzled him, too. All Mia wanted was her connection to Ty to wash away the residue of the visit from Bri. She loosened Ty's tie and hung his jacket up, getting him a glass of ginger ale and cranberry juice. "Sweetheart?" Mia said softly, handing him the glass.

"Ok, now I know something is up. I know that '*sweetheart*'," Ty laughed, wishing she'd unmask the reasons behind such niceties.

"Ah ite, ah ite..I wanna leave next weekend - this anticipation is gonna burst something in me," she told him. Ty paused, threw himself back on the lounge and smiled. "Baby, please!" Mia pleaded, hugging his neck from behind. "Well, if it dries your tears and keeps that smile on your face…I'll make it do what it do, baby!" Ty said, in hIS favorite Ray Charles voice.

Ty immediately contacted his personal secretary to re-arrange their travel itinerary for an earlier departure. His assistant, Ingrid Johannsen, was a loyal confidante of Dutch and Scottish descent, whom Ty had met during his freshman year at Boston University. Ingrid was the only person privy to all of Ty's personal, financial and business affairs. He'd convinced her to stay at Boston U instead of returning to Amsterdam when homesickness and high tuition interfered in her schooling. Undoubtedly, Ty's initial interest had something to do with her striking 5'9" figure and looks that could grace the cover of Vogue. Ty had always been open to cultural exploration and was drawn to her international flair. He lent her his own Pell Grant monies throughout their undergrad years, and he later convinced her to apply and join him at Harvard. She finished her MBA at Harvard Business School while Ty attended Harvard Law. They'd been together ever since, and she'd became his most trusted adviser. She settled in the Midwest to work for him. It was Ingrid who taught Ty the intricacies of a woman's thought processes and of romance. Both were equally fond of each other, yet found it awkward, after so many years, to rise from the intimacy-void of the

148

"Friend Zone." Ingrid knew how important this trip was to Ty, so she helped stage a meticulous adventure, filled with romance, excitement and intrigue. One of her favorite sayings was that "a trip falls short in one's memory, but a journey circles the heart forever.' She phoned Ty after completing the arrangements. "Tyson, everything is a go – I think you will both be thoroughly pleased," Ingrid reported.

"I swear I'm gonna name my first daughter Ingrid – you're one in a million!" Ty expressed his gratitude.

Mia waited anxiously for his confirmation of the travel arrangements. With her hands glued to the phone, it didn't take but half a ring before she picked up Ty's phone call. "Hello, wassup, babe?" Mia asked.

Sounding exhausted and disappointed Ty sighed, "Look sweetie…" after a slight pause, "I tried everything and I came up with…," Ty stuttered, feigning the impending bad news.

"Bay-bee, they said no?" Mia's comforting tone was tinged with disappointment.

"Well, I made them an offer they couldn't refuse," Ty growled.

"What?" Mia was confused.

"I told them I'd give my kidney and piece of liver to make it happen, but I couldn't give my heart because you already had it!"

At that, Mia smiled. "Yeah right, there go that game!" she told him.

"Did it work?" Ty asked in jest.

"Umm, yeah…boy, you crazy!" Mia responded, her voice a submissive wow.

"Pack your bags. We're takin' our romantic, comedy-thriller on the road," Ty said, eliciting a joyous scream from the other end of the phone,

"Yesss!" Since Ty had rearranged their travel, Pam was no longer privy to their plans. Ty, never one to underestimate Bri or his reach, nor the propensity of friends to betray when gifts were dangled in front of them, asked Mia to keep their plans secret from all, including Pam. He understood that the one thing more indomitably evil than greed was jealousy. In just forty-eight hours, Ty and Mia could escape into to the freedom of not having to steal away. They would become proprietors of their moments together; a free flowing channel of bliss, a bottomless well of love to quench their parched hearts.

CHAPTER XVII

Italy Bound

The day of their departure came as a white Christmas morn. Mia opened her drapes to hurry the rising of the sun and affirm the reality of the day. As Ty had asked, Mia had packed light, allowing room for a spree abroad and expediting exit and entry through customs. The flights were scheduled to depart St. Louis Lambert International Airport at 10:15 a.m., and Mia, still living with her mother, was to meet Ty inside Terminal A. He had instructed her to arrive early and board the plane immediately after clearing the gate. Ty would enter at the very last moment. He was taking every precaution to safeguard not only their secrecy of the affair, but Mia's safety as well.

Mia rushed to answer the familiar knock at the door, but instead of Ty, she met a chauffeur dressed in traditional escort garb, waiting to escort her to the limousine out front. It was these unexpected, spontaneous touches that kept Mia off balance and amazed at how Ty uniquely showed his affection. As Mia exited, she disconnected the battery from her cell phone, disabling the GPS tracking devices. Inside the limo, an array of stargazer lilies and African violets lined the floorboards and seats. A chilled glass of '68 Chateau de Montaigne stood aside a tray of berries, mango and her favorite, chocolate cake. Mia was greeted with a polite nod from a uniformed masseuse, a slight young woman of Thai descent. The tinted windows and interior lights lent the feel of dusk, as Gato Barbieri's "*Europa*" surrounded her softly. A TV screen slowly descended from the ceiling, and as Ty appeared on the screen, the

151

music dimmed to a backdrop.

"Hey babe, I can't wait to see you, relax and enjoy….see you soon!" Ty said, "Oh, yeah….take off your shoes." Kicking them off on his cue, Mia relaxed as the masseuse kneeled and with warm lavender oil, began massaging her feet. The thirty-minute ride was its own tiny getaway, and as the tension left her, the anticipation of what lay ahead tingled Mia's senses as she longing to see what was next. Still unaware of their destination, Mia reached the airport, hurrying through checkout with nothing but a carry-on and her purse. Mia proceeded to the gate, where the screen above the counter read Philadelphia. "Okaaay…Philly?" she thought. "Well, it's a getaway!" She knew that if Philly was the place, Ty would make it feel like Paris in the spring. Mia tucked her bag overhead and took her seat the second row of first class. Nervously, she waited for Ty to board. When she heard, "this is the final boarding for Flight 1003 to Philadelphia. Cabin, turn off all electronic devices and prepare for takeoff," Mia stood up to summon the flight attendant. "Ma'am, excuse me, but there's another – " But she stopped as Ty strode through the cabin door. A smile of relief lit up her face, and she clutched Ty's hands as he sat.

Laying her hand atop of his lap and head comfortably on his shoulder, "So what, you takin' your home girl to Philly? I've never been there," Mia said, as Ty simply smirked. "What's that for?" What do you have up your sleeve?" Mia prodded him. Once again, he simply flashed an indecipherable smile, kissed her on the cheek and closed his eyes to nap.

Two restful hours later, "we're making our final descent into Philadelphia, please prepare the cabin for landing." the Captain announced.

Mia stretched to get her bag from the overhead compartment, and tried to jostle Ty awake.

"For those deplaning in Philadelphia, please enjoy your stay in the City of Brotherly Love. Those continuing on to Cagliari, Sardinia, please relax . We'll ready the aircraft and be taking off shortly." Pre-occupied with her luggage in the hopes of beating exiting passengers off the plane, the second part of the travel announcement didn't register with Mia. When she shook Ty's shoulder again, he opened his eyes and smiled furtively, grabbing her leg, signaling her to hold. "E cosi ti piace la Sardegna? Primo fermata!" Ty asked, in his limited and broken Italian. "So you like Sardinia? First stop!" Mia's jaw dropped as she realized what was behind his smirks. Sardinia was their destination. Cagliari was a mountainous capitol port city in northeast Sardinia. It was situated west of Italy and due south of Corsica. Its beauty was similar to the Arcadian village of Tivoli, Mia's birthplace and childhood home. Ty's itinerary took through Cagliari to St. Theresa in Northern Sardinia and across the Strait of Bonifacio for three days on the private isle of Ile Cavallo, a French territory to the southeast. Mia's dream was to once more taste Italy, and Ty knew that Sardinia would delight her soul. What he didn't tell her about was his plan to charter a flight across the Tyrrhenian Sea from Ile Cavallo onto the mainland of Italy, just a step away from Tivoli. For now, she and Ty would savor the moment, enjoying the eight hour international flight in first class and each other's company, with no fear and no worry.

First class provided luxury and decadence, with exquisite cuisine – eggplant parmesan, orange-pecan encrusted Chilean sea bass and asparagus with ratatouille cream sauce, and an array of international desserts. They toasted the moment with a wine from Missouri's Augusta wineries, and snuggled together to watch the in-flight movie, "The Notebook," a mutual favorite. They both found it symbolic of their own love story, with its familiar, timeless depth and the understanding that destiny was too often misdiagnosed as coincidence. As they flew over the Mediterranean, the cabin was bathed in darkness, lit only by the aisle guides. When a turbulent lurch awakened her, Mia stared at a sleeping Ty, still amazed at her fortune. She was as clay, to be molded into whatever his hands imagined. Open and vulnerable, Mia felt safe in his presence. Ty's confidence was not a swagger like Bri's but a head held high. His soft charm and how he creatively fulfilled the longings of her mind, body and spirit rendered void any lingering inhibition. She shined a smile of devilish innocence and grabbed the rise of his pants, softly stroking him as she stood up, staring intensely with a soft, but focused gaze as if to say, "Come on!" Her ocular invitation became almost a dare, and Ty's boyish smile affirmed he understood Mia's and the spontaneous invitation to fulfill a fantasy and join the Mile High Club.

International flights provided the best in space and accommodation, making a public tryst all the more intriguing. Ty followed Mia from first class toward the rear of the plane. The attendants and proximity to the cockpit made the forward section unrealistic for their exploits. They found a rear row in an emergency aisle that afforded a greater recline, and nervously scanned the immediate area one last time. Mia covered Ty's lap with her blanket, laying her head inconspicuously underneath. She unzipped his pants, exposing just enough of Ty to navigate around it with her hands and then lips. Mia, now in charge, commanded Ty as her apprentice, putting her all into her efforts, fulfilling for him a most treasured fantasy. Bringing Ty to the brink with nowhere to release, Mia lay lip-locked around him, bringing his climax to the fore. Mia's temperature still read hot and combustible, as measured by the warm moisture that saturated her walls. Rejuvenating Ty's rise reciprocally tamed her own fiery coals. Her determination succeeded as Ty rose and pulled her quickly to the restroom. Mia had secretly planned ahead, removing her panties before flight. Once inside, Mia locked the door and propped herself on the sink, spreading her legs. "You wanna taste? Indulge!" Mia invited, in her most sultry tone. Ty dropped to his knees, spread her lips to expose her clit and obliged her request to wet his palate with a taste of her, and savored every bit of moisture that flowed between her limbs.

Feeling her clitoris tense and her abdomen tighten, Ty withdrew his tongue and slowly guided his fullness into her, alternating deep and shallow thrusts. They were interrupted by a knock on the door. Ty covered her mouth as her moans were becoming louder. The knock only heightened the intensity of this pleasurable, forbidden moment of spontaneity. Their bodies met with rhythmic thrusts until Mia's legs dropped, trembling from her climactic implosion of joy. Still clenched and breathing heavily, they smiled deeply into each other's eyes, knowing they'd fulfilled a fantasy beyond expectations. They walked out of the restroom separately but only by seconds. Sitting just one row away, a young Italian flight attendant smiled, giving a subtle nod of approval at this rare display of American sexual liberty. Situated comfortably back in their seats, they toasted glasses of Aveleda Fonte Vinho Verde wine. "To this moment and all that follow!" Ty said lifting his glass.

"To us!" Mia exclaimed happily, meeting his glass in toast as they savored the remaining moments before their final leg into Sardinia. They were thrilled by the sight of the Gibraltar Rock, resting between the northern coast of Morocco and the southern tip of Spain in the Strait of Gibraltar at the entrance to the Mediterranean. The

155

spectacle was no less intoxicating as the sun dropped toward the horizon against such a beautiful backdrop. "Have you ever seen such beauty?" Ty asked, as he continued to marvel at the glorious scene. "Not since the first sunset we watched at Kiener Plaza," Mia smiled, memorializing their first unofficial date. As their flight approached Cagliari Airfield, Ty joyfully serenaded Mia with a line from Prince's "*International Lover.*"

"Welcome to Cagliari, Sardinia. We hope you enjoyed your flight and enjoy your stay," the Captain announced as the plane taxied the runway. They boarded a shuttle on the tarmac for the hour transit to Hotel Calamosca, where Ty had booked a suite. The drive was a journey through the most scenic areas of Sardinia's southern coast to the southeastern tip of Capo Carbonara, 35 miles from Cagliari. The route illuminated the simple serenity of a hidden town, self-sufficient and independent of the excessive material trappings. On the outskirts of Cagliari, local townsmen in traditional dress lined the stone corridors between quaint domiciles, courtship in the air. The men might as well have puffed out their chests, and flexed their biceps as subtle as they were in auditioning for the attention of the beautiful Sardinian belles. Mia let out a sigh of utter delight, wondering if this might have been the inspiration for the cover of a romance novel. It seemed a natural habitat for their growing love. With a solemn glance, she turned to Ty, "Would you ever live in such a place?"

"Only if you graced my stay with your lifelong presence," Ty smiled, planting a gentle kiss of the back of her hand.

Home Alone

Back in St. Louis, Bri had become increasingly agitated at his inability to reach Mia. She had always, without question, been accessible and willing to sacrifice to satisfy his infatuation with big toys and lofty dreams. Now he found himself unable to get legal releases for loan documentation on their residence. The 10,000 sq. ft. home in Huntleigh Manor had been twice mortgaged to satisfy the debt Bri incurred through various business ventures and his notorious gambling habit. Mia's worth had never registered as high as in her absence now. Bri sat motionless on the chaise where he and Mia had often cuddled at the start of their relationship, staring at their wedding picture on the nearby table. "What the hell am I doing…shit is slowly slipping away," he thought to himself as he sipped on a glass of Louis VIII de Remy Martin cognac. The home, marriage, business, reputation and friends, that had always come so easily, seemed to be fading from his grasp. As his mind took this inventory, he felt weakened at the very core. He'd never viewed himself as ordinary, because he'd always avoided the luxury of emotion. He'd believed that emotions were the antithesis to survival and domination, yet Mia's absence was stirring up a noticeable void. Which, naturally, boiled over into a stew of rage at Tyson Penn. To restore order to his world, Bri knew he had to work Mia back into the fold. He didn't know where they were, but being blind-sided by their getaway moving up to two weeks added the fuel of envy to his rageful fire. He tried tracking her phone, but got nothing, which made no sense. She always kept her phone on. Bri attempted to reach Ty, but his calls went straight to voicemail. Hanging up in frustration, he decided to phone Mia's mother not caring that she'd never done a very good job of hiding her disdain for him.

One of Savita's favorite movies was Sparkle, and she'd always believed that Bri's hold over Mia was much like that of the beautiful, beaten and oppressed heroine. For a time, Bri had succeeded in alienating Mia from her family, until she finally left him and returned to the safety of their arms.

Tonight's call was met with equal disdain. Mrs. Whitmore hesitated to pick up the phone when she saw his number. As it continued ringing, she said to herself, "If Davis was alive, this joker would be six feet under." So she waited, and the ringing finally stopped.

Bri was now forced to contact the only other person he believed would know of Mia's whereabouts, Pam. Bri had Pam on speed dial. "Hey, what's up, baby girl? How ya movin'?" he asked. Pam never let the phone ring twice when Bri called.

"What?" How you wan' a sista to move, Pimpin'?" Pam teased him, hoping he'd hear her continuing hope to ride or die with him.

That was the inch that Bri needed to take his mile. "Why don't you roll over here, I wanna run something past you?" Bri asked.

"What? Somethin' past me or in me?" Pam retorted with a smirk. Bri chuckled, and then gave a sharp-toned directive, "Look, one hour, be here!" He hung up. He did wonder, *"Trick, if she'd do this to her best friend, what the hell would she do to me?"* He needed her though, so he let that curse go as quickly as he'd thought it, and re-focused on his current concern. He considered the million dollar policy he'd taken out on Mia's life. Bri decided it would be the quickest way to satisfy his personal debt and the street bounties that would surface if those debts weren't paid. He called his insurance carrier. "Hello, this is Brandon Baptiste, checking on account LZ510730 for Mia Farone Whitmore. I want to send a payment,"

Bri said he told the customer service rep.

"I'm sorry sir, this policy has lapsed. Mrs. Whitmore will need to contact her agent and re-sign a policy in order to reestablish the account, then you can pay," the operator instructed Bri. There was a notation on the policy at Mia's request that any attempt to alter the account required her to be notified. She had long ago become skeptical of her future with Bri, and the separation and his mounting debt forced her to hold the policy in her name only.

Pam rang his door bell just as Bri hung up from the agent. He switched into auto-charm. "Hey, what's up, baby girl? I'm glad you could make it," Bri smiled, as he planted a light kiss on her cheek. Without effort on Bri's part to extract information, Pam opened up like a six-lane highway ready to be rolled. But Bri was about the business first. "Now baby, I wanna trust you, I do. You know getting' a man like me is like hittin' the lottery....ya digg?

"But I think you got the ticket," Bri said holding her face between his palms. Starry-eyed, as if she'd made the final cut of a casting call, she slowly nodded her head, anticipating marching orders like a good army recruit. Bri had already acknowledged, after the phone call with the insurance agent, that expecting Mia to sign anything for him, especially a promissory note on her life, was exceedingly unrealistic. Having virtually no time to spare, he asked Pam to forge Mia's name on a piece of important paperwork. He insisted she refrain from asking any questions, and faked a show of a rare moment of trust and vulnerability by telling he the forms were for a home policy about to lapse. He told her he planned to have the house burned down and collect on the policy, and promised to set Pam up like a princess.

"Baby, I just wanna start over. I wanna burn the memories of my past to ash and move forward… with someone who appreciates me," Bri told her, insinuating who that might be. Pam wound her arms around his neck, making sure he knew she would happily oblige his overtures.

"First thing is…I need to find out where Mia is, so we won't bump heads on this," Bri told Pam. Pam offered to visit Mia's mother under the guise of checking on her. Mrs. Whitmore knew Pam as her daughter's long-time friend and confidante and had no reason to suspect hidden motives. Mrs. Whitmore was just a shadow of the young Italian belle who'd first came to America from Italy almost 30 years earlier, yet her beauty was unfettered. When she opened the door, "Hello, Ma Whitmore!" Pam greeted her affectionately.

"Hello Pamela, how are you?" Mrs. Whitmore answered.

"I'm fine, how you doin'? Sorry to just stop by, but I promised Mia I would send her a package; do you know where can I reach her?" Pam asked.

"Oh, honey, she landed in Sardinia just a few days ago!" Mrs. Whitmore jubilantly exclaimed. Even though she had never approved of any relationship outside marriage, she had taken an immense liking to Ty and how happy Mia was with him. Pam felt slighted, wondering why Mia had not confided in her. The hurt feelings added justification to her decision to align herself with Bri. "Well, Ma Whitmore, I just wanted to check on you - love you!" Pam's warm hug belied her growing callousness.

"Sardinia?" Pam thought. "Where the hell is that?" Geography had never been her strong suit. Once clear of Mrs. Whitmore, she

160

phoned Bri with the news.

"Hello?" Bri answered.

"Sardinia!" Pam responded hurriedly, forgoing a proper greeting.

"Sar-what? What are you talking about?"Bri growled with agitation.

"Sardinia, it's overseas – somewhere near Europe, I think." Pam answered unintelligently.

"Ah ite, good looking out, I get back at you in a minute," Bri told her, hanging up before she could respond.

CHAPTER XVIII

Return to Tivoli

Ty and Mia landed at Rome's Ciampico Airport, and Mia's racing emotions condensed into bright tears as they headed out along the very roads her parents had once traveled. Much had changed in Italy since Mia was a child, but the countryside had been frozen in time. The rugged, unpaved roadways leading into Tivoli from Rome were scarcely populated except for a few privately-owned farms and the farmhands who worked the olive groves. Alongside the roads sat wooden cottages, missing the amenities of modern living. Nevertheless, life looked peaceful without the stresses and burdens of a concrete jungle, which seems to enslave inhabitants to the material trappings of success.

Ty marveled at the simple harmony between nature and the people as they moved about in their work and play. The scent of olives wafted on the breeze, and with each mile closer to Tivoli, a medley of sorrow, joy and happiness bubbled in Mia's mind. Ty sat quietly, watching the tears stream down Mia's face as she stared out the carriage window, unsure how to comfort her, not knowing what had drawn the tears. He grabbed her hand, rubbing it with assurance. "You know he's here, smiling on you, Mia Flower!" Ty said. Mia Flower was the name that her father had affectionately called her. Mia smiled, grateful for not only his words, but his presence.

"Thanks babe, I know," she said laying her head on his shoulder as her tears subsided. As she stared up at Ty as his watched the serenity of the passing countryside, the realization hit her. She was drawn to this man because he was so much like her father. The stories her mother had told her throughout her life were reborn with Ty.

Her father's love had been returned to her through Ty. The 17-mile stretch from the countryside of Rome to the center of Tivoli replicated the romantic origins of her parents' transit. Mia lay comfortably in Ty's arms, her silence filled with gratitude. In the closeness and security, she felt her tears of sorrow evaporate and morph into giddy excitement knowing that Tivoli sat just over the horizon. 'Tivoli –20 kilometers," the sign read, and Mia could hardly contain her enthusiasm. About 50 yards away, she saw a billboard that read, 'CAVALI OLIVES…A LITTLE TASTE OF ITALY.' "Wow, stop here!" Mia exclaimed out of the blue.

"What's wrong, baby?" Ty worried, grabbing hold of her as he sensed the urgency in her voice. Mia climbed out of the carriage and ran toward the sign. Ty held her hand, bewildered, but followed her lead. "Cavali Oil was where my father worked! The man in the picture is Carmine Lucci, the owner. He's the most respected man in Tivoli, and his daughter was my best friend!" Mia explained to Ty, full of affection for the man known as Don Lucci. The affection sprang from memories of her mother and hundreds of townspeople celebrating along the parade route, honoring his return from his extended prison stay in Sardinia. Her heart raced as she thought of Nadia, wondering if Nadia would even remember her now.

Arriving in Tivoli's municipal center, the couple was energized by the vibrancy and life. The central square had the cosmopolitan flare of New York's Greenwich Village, the edges of which had been smoothed by sincere southern hospitality.

Ty, known for his spontaneity, blended a meticulous attention to detail and planning, with a far reaching thoughtfulness that would shake Mia's core and astound her. If they did nothing more from now on but watch the setting of the sun, Mia's heart would be full. Simply seeing Tivoli again filled her with eternal gratitude. "Look, babe, there's my old school!" Mia shouted over the bustle, immediately thrust back in time to holding her father's hand, skipping with Nadia through childhood. She was pummeled by conflicting yet complementary emotions as the memories swirled.

"Is that where all the girls not as pretty as you took your lunch money?" Ty joked.

"Nawwwh, Joker! Nadia always had my back. I wonder where she's at now?" Mia asked in reminiscent wonder. Their carriage stopped in front of the Villa Plauzi, a small, chic hotel, located near the revered fountains and gardens of the Villa d'Este. Ty hoped to temper Mia's curiosity before she began prompting him to expose his cards.

"Babe, I want you to relax and let me be your guide," Ty gently asserted, kissing her before departing the carriage into the hotel. "Buon serra, Mi chiamo Tyson Penn, la stanza per deux," Ty introduced himself, requesting their reservation from at the front desk. The clerk was smitten by Ty's elementary use of Italian.

"Buonsera, Monsieur Penn, piacere!" the blushing clerk returned the afternoon greeting and handed him the keys to Room 330. Ty loaded up their bags, and when Mia opened the room door, he dropped the load of bags, throwing himself across the bed as Mia threw herself over him.

Grinning, Mia kissed him from cheek to cheek and planted one on his forehead. "Baby, I love you so much...thank you!" St. Louis was as far from her mind as the miles of ocean that separated the continents. Ty knew he couldn't rest long before setting his surprises in motion.

He ran a hot tub of bubbly water for Mia, relaxation the perfect diversion. He lit candles and placed chocolate biscotti and a miniature bottle of wine he'd scored on their flight near the tub for her. He led her from the bed to the tub, "Here babe, rest your body and I'll fire it up later...gotta run downstairs," Ty said, and was gone with a wink.

Childhood Reunion

At the front desk, Ty requested use of the phone. "The phone service is not set up for outgoing international calls," the clerk informed him.

"No ma'am, it's local," he said, dialing the number he'd copied onto a note card. "02-01-11-1947," Ty said to himself as he dialed. The phone rang three times and then, "Ciao!" a woman answered.

"Nadia Lucci?" Ty asked.

"Si," she replied. "Who wants to know?"

"This is Tyson Penn, Mia Farone Whitmore's friend; we spoke about a month ago."

"Yes!" she replied enthusiastically.

"Mia and I are in Tivoli and she has already asked about you," Ty said.

The line went silent while Nadia gained her composure. She, like Mia, had always reminisced of her best friend, never imagining she would ever see her again. No friendship in the 25 years they'd been apart had ever paralleled the depth of theirs. "I'm in Milan now, but I'll be back in Tivoli tomorrow afternoon. Why don't we meet at the stone bench on the east side of the schoolyard, maybe just before sunset?" Nadia said.

"Great!" Ty exclaimed. He'd heard stories about their bench, the spot where Nadia and Mia had spent considerable time before and after school. They'd chiseled their names in the stone, which sat

166

near what was now the Lucci Montessori Scuola, renamed for Nadia's father after Mia had left Tivoli. Ty had reached out to Nadia after a two-week search for her, because he knew the importance of their relationship and couldn't imagine a finer gift for Mia than granting her lifelong wish of returning to Tivoli and finding her best friend.

Mia was still soaking in the bubbles, mellowed from the fragrant lavender and vanilla caliente' candle and wine. Ty massaged her feet and softly nibbled her toes, alternating between hand and mouth. "Oooh, bay-bee, what took you so long?" Mia asked with her thumb sensuously resting on her lips. Something about Tivoli lit the fiery passion of intense erotica. Or maybe her desire had been deepened by Ty's selfless acts of love. Either way, his mere presence was an orgasmic precursor. "I bet you an orgasm that you can't lay inside me without moving for five minutes!" Mia teasingly wagered the seductive suction of her lips around him, only if he could achieve such a feat insider her throbbing, wet love well without moving or exploding the love lava of his longing.

"Bet dat, young woman!" he smiled.

"Ah ite, keep up old man!" she said, climbing out of the tub, leaning her mouth toward his peak with her tongue outstretched, only to stop at his tip to blow warm, wet air around it, teasing and heightening his tension to close out the wager quickly.

"Ahhhh, ah ite…you're playing dirty!" Ty said, spreading her over the bed, outstretching her arms. Teasing her in return, Ty barely circled her breast with his tongue, his breath warm on her skin as his knees stretched her thighs open to their limit. His fingers rotated the upper reaches of her clit, intensifying her longing for him to move

167

inside her. Ty made his scintillating southern descent, stopping to cool her fiery coals with the moist compression of his tongue, bringing her to the brink of erogenous ecstasy. He stood up, detaching himself from the moment, leaning back with his handle completely erect and perpendicular to his body, and slowly stroked himself, inviting Mia to take hold.

"Ummh, ummh, hell naw, you ain't gonna do it like that!" Mia smiled, understanding that this had now become a contest of sexual wills. She grabbed him, increasing her hand rotation around his shaft and placed it inside her mouth as she rotated her own middle finger over her clit like it was powered by a D cell battery. She hummed and moaned on him as he watched her lower lips palpitate. Sensing Ty was primed for release and that his body was now fully relaxed, she guided him inside her. "Now remember, you can't move," Mia whispered seductively in his ear, one hand firmly grasping his lower back and the other his ass.

"Dammit!" Ty said remembering the wager and realizing that he'd been erotically outfoxed. Mia continued teasing him by flexing her vaginal muscles until Ty could no longer maintain his resistance and remain still. Rising up on his chiseled arms, he thrust inside of her until he burst like a jack-legged levee.

"Game over, pay up!" Mia said, as Ty lay on his back across the bed as if he'd just gone ten rounds with Mike Tyson. When he appeared unable to answer the bell, Mia straddled directly spread over his face. "Welcome to Tivoli, you like Italian?" Mia said lowering her dripping pussy over his mouth, cupping his head to lock his tongue in her groove. Ty happily obliged, holding her arms firm and fixed, so she couldn't escape the intense explosion of her own erotic-atomic bomb. Like two battle-worn soldiers in a ditch, they lay in each other's arms for the next hour and a half. They finally arose, showered and decided to cap off their first night in Tivoli with a stroll along the banks of the Aniene River. Morning had come, the sun streaming through the sheer drapes. The light, sounds of accordion music playing outside and the smell of ambrosia and macchiato awakened Mia, as Ty sat at the side of the bed, greeting her with a smile of latent bliss. "Buongiorno, Signor Tyson Penn!" she returned his smile with a subtle kiss.

"Come on sweetie, we have a busy morning and a few surprises," Ty said.

"Oh, really? What?" Mia quizzed with a sigh, knowing full well that Ty would not reveal. Her anticipation energized her, even more so than the cup of dark roasted macchiato she sipped. She nibbled the coconut and orange slices of the ambrosia as they readied themselves for the taxi, and Ty blindfolded Mia as they took off in the cab. "I don't know if you're crazy or I'm crazy for letting you do this," she laughed. Just a short distance from the hotel, they stopped. The cab driver opened her door as Ty took her hand, leading her to the sidewalk in front of a humble, but neatly charming abode. "All right!" Ty said, removing the blindfold.

Mia stared, her hands jumping to the sides of her face as she took it in. "How did you know?" Mia turned to ask as his arms circled her from behind.

"Love helps you find a way," he smiled, as they gazed at her childhood home. The home of her grandmother had been handed down to her mother; structurally it was seemed unchanged from twenty-five years ago, with the exception of new paint and sidewalks. Mia recalled so many joyous times, her father pushing

169

her on demand in the swing he'd hung from the tree in the back of the house, the delightful smells of her mother's cooking. "Come on!" Ty interrupted her roaming thoughts.

"Where?" she asked. Ty led her by hand through the yard to the front door.

"Wait! Boy, are you crazy?" Mia said, stunned at Ty's brazen attempt to knock on a stranger's door. As she spoke, an elderly woman opened the door and walked slowly to the edge of the porch. "Tyson? Mia?" the woman queried.

The woman's familiarity drew a puzzled look from Mia, who wondered how she knew their names. "Yes, Ms. Fratelli, how are you?" Ty bowed and clasped her hand in response, and Mia realized Ty and the elderly woman were co-conspirators in this surprise.

"You don't know me, but I knew your mother and father. Davis and Savita sold me this house when you left for America. Good family, good man," she said. The compliment soothed Mia and brought on a smile. "How is your dear mother?" Ms. Fratelli asked.

"Fine, she's just fine. Thanks for asking!" Mia responded, still in wonder.

"Come in, please. Would you two like some floral tea and biscotti?" Ms. Fratelli offered. Biscotti seemed to be the standard Italian snack, like a chocolate chip cookie with a regal flair. Adapting quickly to the hospitable nature of Tivoli, Ty and Mia made themselves comfortable.

"Hey, I wanna show you something," Ty said to Mia, as if he'd been there before. He hadn't, of course, but he had paid particular attention, taking detailed mental notes every time Mia and her mother reminisced. It was a quality that endeared her to him. Ty took her to a tree out back. She had mentioned it to him ages ago in a conversation about her childhood, but at this moment, seemed mystified. The tree was a monument her father had planted for her, and when it had grown strong enough, he'd carved the words, "Daddy's Mia Flower," which had weathered time and the elements and was still legible.

"Oh my goodness, it's,"…Mia began.

Ty interrupted. "I remember every word that falls from your beautiful lips!" he said. Ty stepped back to give her space, as Mia knelt, rubbing her hand over the engraved words as she began to cry. She could vividly picture her father planting the tree as she played alongside, and later carving those words. Her mind's eye focused on her father sneaking her favorite candy, against her mother's wishes, and hiding it behind the tree. In awe, she realized again how similar Ty was to her father, his nurturing, caring ways so mirrored her Dad's.

Two o'clock had approached, and Ty gathered Mia to leave after they obliged the hospitality of Ms. Fratelli. They promised to come back as they thanked her for her kindness.

Unfulfilled by the calorie-deprived biscotti, they walked to Caffe Letterario, a sandwich shop just three blocks away and directly across the street from the school. After finishing the lamb and feta brioche, a soft Italian pastry that Mia loved, they walked seemingly without aim, guided only by the compass of laughter toward the east side of the school yard to the stone bench. "Can we sit for a minute?" Ty prompted. Mia had spoken often of her school days and the playground by which they now sat but was unaware of its particular significance on this day. Maybe overwhelmed by all that being back in Tivoli meant to her, maybe overcome with the memories of her childhood home, she let her thoughts ramble, sharing each memory with Ty as it popped into her head. Ty was listening attentively to Mia's verbal journey down Tivoli's memory lane when a poodle, leash in tow, trotted toward the bench to inspect these newcomers. "Awww, here puppy, puppy," Mia whistled to draw the poodle near.

"It's adorable!" Mia said turning her attention to cuddle the well-groomed dog and his tag that read 'Chi Chi'.

Echoes of "Chi Chi, Chi Chi!" rang across the school yard as a young, chic woman, with oversized Chanel sunglasses and a gorgeous scarf covering long, silken hair followed the dog in their direction.

The dog sat in Mia's lap as the woman continued to call for Chi Chi. "Here, here she is!" Mia called out. Ty sat quietly, barely able to contain himself because he knew who was approaching them.

"Ah, thank you! My Chi Chi seems to know this bench is a treasured monument of sorts for my dear, lost friend and me," she said. Mia paused, wondering of the possibility of such a coincidence. "Naww!" she thought to herself. As she turned away, the woman hummed a tune eerily similar to a song Mia and Nadia had sung together as children. Turning back, she lifted her sunglasses from her eyes. "Mia, Mia, congalia, Mia Mia" she sang, affirming the breathtaking coincidence. "Na -dia, Dia, congalia, Dia, Dia!" Mia sang back to her. They ran to embrace, circling and jumping up and down like the kindergartners they once were.

172

Mia realized almost instantly that this meeting had not happened by chance. "Let me guess, this is no coincidence, huh?" Mia asked, looking at Nadia and Ty.

"Surprise, babe!" Ty said, as Mia joyfully nudged him.

"So, I assume I don't need to introduce you to my guy?" Mia grinned at Nadia, simultaneously glancing knowingly at Ty. This was the first time that either was comfortable acknowledging publically that they were a couple. Any remnants of a relationship with Bri hung only by the legal thread of matrimony.

"Ah, yes, and kudos to you for your taste! Ty was very determined and persistent to make this trip perfect for you." Nadia said, smiling at Ty.

"Look, I want to take you two on a tour of the New Tivoli, but first I want to stop by my parents' house," Nadia told them. A black, deeply-tinted Audi sedan pulled up to the gate, as the driver's window slid down. "Hey, Nadia, I see you've found what you were looking for," the young Italian man said.

"Mia, Ty. This is Carlo, my brother," Nadia introduced him.

"No way, I remember he was just a little toddler when I left!" Mia laughed.

Carlo was stoic; his gentlemanly upbringing allowed only the smallest of smiles and a brief greeting, "Buon sera!" Carlo was a departure from the sophistication and joviality of his feared, loved and respected father. They all piled into his car for the drive to the outskirts of the town to meet Nadia's parents, Vitalia and Carmine Lucci, who were unaware of Mia's presence in Tivoli. For both,

173

seeing her would surely dredge up memories – fatal memories - for both the Luccis.

For the moment, though, the backseat could barely contain the joy of the girls' reunion. Nadia and Mia chatted endlessly, the years washed away by their bond. In stark contrast, Carlo and Ty sat silently in the front seat. Carlo's nature, as the only son of Don Carmine Lucci, led him to distrust strangers, especially this close to the heir to his father's throne. But he knew this visit was important to his sister, Nadia, whom he adored. He trusted her judgment. Yet Carlo couldn't help but be impressed by Ty's sincerity and humility, as well as the fact that Ty seemed quite comfortable, not intimidated by his stature. Carlo inwardly applauded Ty's efforts and travels for Mia. His love for her must run quite deep. Nadia phoned home, "Papa, are you and Mama home?" she asked her father.

"No Nadi, we're at the cabin in Naples until this evening, why?" he answered.

"I just wanted to see you. Can we meet for breakfast tomorrow? I have a surprise," she said.

"Sure, Nadi, sure!" he replied. This suited Ty, because he had other plans for the evening.

Ty wanted to trace the steps of Mia's parents' courtship and her earlier life in Tivoli. Nadia and Carlo dropped Ty and Mia off at the hotel. "We will pick you up for breakfast in the morning," Nadia said.

"Great!" Mia replied.

"Ok, Carlo, piacere!" Ty said, drawing a chuckle from Carlo. He saw, in Ty's attempt at Italian, a sign of respect for Italy and its culture.

"Si, Ciao!" Carlo responded as they pulled away.

"I'm afraid to ask what you have planned for us tonight," Mia chuckled, still blown away by the many unexpected joys she'd experienced so far.

"Why don't we go upstairs so that you can change? You can model that dress for me and then for all of Tivoli!" Ty said, as they stood in the lobby, arm in arm, waiting for the elevator to their room.

The evening's first stop was the Teatro Don Bosco, a cinema that doubled as a playhouse, where "La Boehme," Puccini's most famous opera, was playing. Even though Mia's childhood of classical music had been augmented by the sounds of Motown; Gaye, Redding, Cooke, Smokey and Jackie, as well as the hip-hop beat of Public Enemy, Eric B and Rakim and BDP, like Tivoli, classical music and opera remained her first loves. Teatro Don Bosco was the theatre her father and mother visited. Their first date had been to the Opera House in Sigonella, by horse and carriage over forty years ago. To modern-day Tivoli, the carriage was no longer a common mode of transit, but was still savored as a travel mode of leisure, a relic of Old Tivoli and its romantic, small countryside mystique. As they waited on the rustic bench outside the hotel, the slow, familiar clacking of horseshoes on cobblestone closed their direction, coming to a halt in front of them. The romantic sight of the two being whisked away in horse and carriage drew the admiration of even the romance-bred Tivolians.

"Remember?" Ty spoke but one word and images of their first

intimate encounter filled Mia's head.

"Yeah, I remember. We made love!" Mia said reverently.

"Made love? Girl, I hit it!" he joked.

"Shut up!" she said, bashfully nudging him. "Yeah, I can't remember if that was you or the horse huffing and gasping for air," Mia shot back jokingly. Her mind was now one hundred percent detached from St. Louis and her problems with Bri. Ty and Tivoli had already become her natural habitat, the happy convergence of desire and fulfillment. Arriving at the theatre, they watched the three-hour opera in deafening silence, and Mia's eyes swelled with tears as the curtains fell.

They remained seated until the last attendee departed the theatre, then Ty walked Mia toward the front. "Come on!" Ty said, hopping onto the stage, offering his hand to Mia.

"What?" Mia replied curiously.

"Alright then…" Ty said, and he belted out a loud yell, mocking the falsetto of the opera performer.

Sparing herself possible further embarrassment from Ty's bold theatrics, "Ah ite, crazy!" she said, giving in and joining him on stage. Making their way through the heavy, velvet stage curtains toward the dressing rooms, Ty looked at the door plate that read "Guiseppe DiFranco," and knocked on the door.

As the opera's star opened the door, Ty introduced Mia as a big fan. "We've come all the way from America to see this production," Ty told him.

"How do you say in America...I am honored." DiFranco said, and bowed to them in gratitude.

"May we bother you for a picture?" Ty asked.

"Of course," he answered, and posed dramatically with Mia.

Leaving the theatre, Ty and Mia walked through the balmy spring night, a subtle breeze brushing their shoulders, along the cobblestone streets at the banks of the river. On the banks, they lay for a short while, Ty's jacket doubling as a blanket so they could find constellations in the night sky.

Then the clacking of horseshoes served notice that it was time to go. A weary Mia rested her head in Ty's lap, unfazed by the jerking of the carriage, blissful, tired and anticipating what the next day would hold. The night passed and, true to her word, Nadia arrived at the front desk of their hotel, prompting the clerk to page them downstairs.

CHAPTER XIX

Meeting Don Carmine

As the beloved daughter of the most respected man in Tivoli, Nadia was closely watched by her brother. Carlo stood ever vigilant by her side, never sacrificing details of security. An enthusiastic Nadia greeted Ty and Mia as they walked down the atrium stairwell with hugs and grins.

"Buon giorno!" a more relaxed Carlo said, extending his hand to greet Ty as Nadia and Mia exchanged the customary cheek-to-cheek welcome. None of them could see the significance ahead of this morning encounter with Don Carmine Lucci, nor the long-buried emotions that would rise to the surface.

Mia's excitement at seeing her best friend's parents again was built on her memories of them from her childhood. For Ty, though, this was to be a remarkable experience because of the stories he'd heard about the fabled Mafioso, Don Carmine Lucci. This meeting would far surpass any of his storied associations of the political elite and street strongman in his circles, even with 'Big Red' Wright. No one was as rich, powerful and authentically Mafioso as Lucci. For Ty, this was humbling and motivating. So many of whom Ty had witnessed in his experiences were cut-throat, renegade, wildcard rogues who were aimless in their criminal pursuits. Such were the criminal elements of the streets. Ty respected the code and order of those given to criminal enterprise, although he himself had never become entrenched. So long as there was honor, respect and loyalty and no collateral harm done to the innocent, he understood the

178

motivation and admired the skill.

Turning from the road, they passed through remote controlled gates into Lucci's estate. They taxied the quarter-mile driveway with manicured bushes along the stretch with awe at its beauty. Foliage draped over the home like a spectacular tablecloth. The mansion was huge and beautiful, but its simplicity underlined the essence of Don Carmine Lucci. His flare was subtle but pronounced, as glorious as the Italian countryside but as simple and common as its inhabitants. Nadia and Carlo circled to the back entrance, escorting Ty and Mia through the kitchen patio into the house. The antique breakfast nook grabbed their attention first. The mosaic tile counter was replete with a breakfast spread of egg, feta and spinach brioche, orange juice, olives and, of course, red wine. In the living room sat Vitalia, Nadia's mother, crocheting. Her long, black hair now flowed with silken strands gray, yet in her aging years, she remained a snapshot of beauty and grace. Don Carmine sat next to her in his recliner, legs stretched over the ottoman, rubbing his faithful feline to the sounds of Gaetano Donizetti's "Lucrezia Borgia." Timidly, Ty and Mia stood tucked behind the wall out of sight, awaiting their introduction. "Papa. Mama. I want you to meet someone," Nadia signaled the two to come out. "This is Mia, remember, my best friend, the daughter of the Farone-Whitmores?" she said. The purring of the cat filled the room.

"Ohhh, my! Mia Farone-Whitmore. You've grown into such a beauty!" Vitalia said graciously, masking her struggle to find appropriate words of welcome.

"And this is her man, Tyson Penn," Nadia added, as she nodded at Ty. Vitalia's greeting disguised the emotions racing through her mind at the memories of Davis, for whom her affection had never

179

faded. Silent, but flashing his charming, warm smile, Don Carmine held out his hand, signaling Mia to come close. Mia grasped his hand, more frail than she expected, as he kissed her palm. He closed his sorrow-filled eyes, as the scene played through his mind, the lifeless body of Mia's father lying in the pool of blood. He could still hear echoes of the burning wood's angry snapping and smell the embers turning to ash. In all the murderous indiscretions of his life, no action ever carried more regret than that of Davis Whitmore, looking into the eyes of Davis' beloved daughter who stood before him. "Of what pain?" he wondered, would come to his own children and wife upon his own death. His eyes involuntarily teared up. No one but Vitalia understood this rare display of emotion or the origins of his sorrow. She'd also been thrust back to the days of the affair and the loss of the precious life for which she'd since held herself responsible.

But to Ty and Mia, innocent of such knowledge, Don Carmine's tears simply showed his elated response to such a joyous welcome. "I remember you as a little girl, your lovely mother…and your hardworking, handsome father. You had no choice but to be beautiful!" the charming Don said. This moment was as awkward for Don Carmine and Vitalia as the moment he first confronted her about Davis nearly thirty years ago. They were both wary of Ty, knowing that sons often exacted revenge for their fathers. "Is this your brother?" Don Carmine asked Mia of Ty.

"No, sir! This is my very dear and beloved friend," Mia answered, flashing a smile at Ty. Later, at the dinner table, Mia shared the story of her life after the death of her father and the challenges of living in America since. The conversation evoked their sympathies as she spoke of her family's alienation from the Black and Italian communities, her abusive and troubling relationship with Bri, and how Ty came into her life and brought joy in the midst of a grave time of self-doubt and mental anguish. She spoke passionately about how he'd reconnected her with love and laughter. If Mia evoked their sympathies, Ty evoked their awe with his support and strength, filling so well the void left by her father's absence. This was a thought that assuaged the guilt of Don Carmine and Vitalia. Carlo, Ty and Don Carmine retreated to the courtyard where the Don gave Ty a few lessons on the game of bocce. "Since it is a game of gentlemen, I will try not to overly celebrate a victory," Ty confidently laughed to the Don as they prepared to play. His sense of humor and confidence amused Don Carmine. "Well young man, I guess this will have to be the Marciano - Louis fight of Bocce!" he chuckled in return, referring to the famous Italian boxing great Rocky Marciano and the African-American boxing great Joe Louis heavyweight bout. Inside, Nadia and Mia talked. Nadia shared her own stories of an abusive relationship and growing up the daughter of one of Italy's most feared and respected men. She had never confided to her parents or Carlo of her own abusive relationship, because she knew it meant certain death for the culprit. Outside, Don Carmine gave a tutorial in Bocce, and chanted, "down goes Louis, down goes Louis!" after soundly beating Ty. Carlo had not seen such a display of vigor and joviality from his father in a long time. Later, the Don sat Ty down alongside Carlo, gifting them both pearls of wisdom on topics from respect to love and business. Hours passed as the conversation stretched into politics, the history of organized crime and its reaches around the globe. Obviously, the Don had taken an immense liking to Ty, who proved himself a humble, sincere and genuine soul. Ty was fascinated, as attentive as an honors student preparing for a final exam. The moment with Don Carmine Lucci was more worthy than a dinner with the President or the Pope. "Poppa, you must rest now." Carlo interrupted the two to give his father a reprieve.

As the women entered the courtyard, Carlo, Ty and Don Carmine stood, bowing with gentlemanly courtesy. As they stood, Don Carmine took the hand of his heir and placed it on top of Ty's to pledge the friendship of his son and the family. Ty knew the gesture was significant, that he was being made an honorary protected member. "And to you, as well, Mia Flower," Don Carmine added, invoking the name her father had called her. The moment her name passed his lips, a soothing sense of vindication filled him, releasing him from his decades of guilt. They left amidst a flurry of farewell kisses and hugs from Don Carmine and Vitalia with promises to visit again very soon. Leaving the estate, they would spend the rest of night and the next few days under the watchful escort of Nadia and Carlo.

Carlo, a young man with a relentlessly judicious eye who found few men up to the high standards he'd inherited from his father, was also impressed with Ty, giving birth to a brotherly bond, underwritten by Don Carmine himself. During their time together, Ty learned that Carlo owned and flew a Piaggio Avanti II plane. With just 48 hours before their flights home, Ty asked Carlo if he could fly everyone down to Reggio di Calabria, a coastal town on the southern tip of Italy, about 250 miles from Tivoli. Initially, Ty wanted to see the island of Monte Cristo, less than 100 miles northwest of Tivoli. Monte Cristo was the island made famous by Alexander Dumas' "the Count of Monte Cristo," a favorite of them both. But it was Reggio di Calabria that Ty found more captivating.

Reggio di Calabria

The foursome boarded the private jet on a landing strip owned by the Luccis behind their parents' home. Comfortably onboard, Carlo, with Ty in the co-pilot's seat, taxied the runway to take off. Ty had frequently ridden shotgun in private planes, but never in a $5 million, Italian-engineered aeronautical masterpiece. As they soared south, Mia phoned her mother back home, filled with enthusiasm and a dying thirst to share her experience thus far. Savita recognized Italy's area code and answered immediately. "Hello! Mia?"

"Mama, how are you doing?" Mia asked.

"I'm fine Mia, how are you?" Savita answered.

"I'm great, Mama! You won't believe it. I'm on a private jet flying over Rome heading to some place called Reggio di Calabria!" Mia said excitedly. "Hold on, Mama, I have a surprise." Mia added, handing the phone to Nadia.

"Hello! Mrs. Farone, this is Nadia, Nadia Lucci," she said.

Savita paused for a moment. "Little Nadia, oh my, how are you, darling?" Savita was pleasantly startled. Mia's mother never held the marital indiscretions of Nadia's mother and her husband against the best friend Mia had in Italy. Mia told her mother of their adventures; the carriage rides, the opera, Ty's backstage theatrics, as well as the visit to their old house. Savita, moved with joy at the elation in her daughter's voice, was taken aback herself, remembering those very same things with Davis. The imitation was certainly flattering; and she was touched, knowing that Ty intentionally set out to retrace their romantic trails for her daughter.

"And, Mama, we spent the day with Nadia's parents at their villa!" Mia exclaimed. "You remember Don Carmine and Vitalia, don't you?" Silence stilled the line as her mother was unable to muster the appropriate response. Although over twenty-five years had passed, the hurt still weighed heavily when it surfaced. "Mama, you hear me?" Mia said breaking the silence.

"Oh yes, Sweetheart, that's great! How are the Luccis?" she asked.

"They're both great and asked of you. Mr. Lucci was solemn but friendly, and he complimented your beauty and mentioned Papa," Mia said.

"What about your Papa?" Savita asked defensively.

"Oh just how hard-working he was and how much he loved me," Mia answered.

Savita didn't allow her own suspicions about why or how Davis had died to dampen Mia's enthusiastic happiness. "That was very kind of the Luccis. How is Tyson?" she asked.

"He's fine!" Mia smiled, as Ty shouted from the cockpit, "Hi, Momma Vita!"

"He's really great, Mama!" she proclaimed, as if making a marketing pitch for Ty. Mia knew that her mother espoused the sanctity of marriage, even if that marriage was miserable. She was all too familiar with the doors that infidelity opened. But even Savita was conflicted over the relationship with Ty, knowing he had lifted her daughter from an abyss of sorrow. She knew Mia's happiness had always been clouded by her father's absence, and she refused to cast a shadow over this sunrise in her daughter's life. "Oh Mama, we're preparing to land, I'll call you later," Mia rushed off the phone.

"Ok, my Mia, be safe, I love you," Savita rung off the line. Carlo, with the ease of riding a bike, descended upon the coastal landing strip tucked between the hills. Reggio di Calabria had been a vital port throughout the Byzantine and Roman Empires, and still maintained a medieval character. For those adept at creative travel, Reggio di Calabria was one of the world's best emerging destinations, an as of yet un-mined European jewel. The warm day and coastal breezes racing over the waters made for a perfect outing. Carlo knew they had only a few hours to taste Reggio before a storm front moved in their direction, so that they could fly out under the rough weather.

Nadia knew just the spot to capture the essence and mystique of this hidden treasure. From the concourse, they took a private cab to the Lungomare, a seaside promenade filled with quaint bars, shops and restaurants. It was ideal for romantic strolls or moments of lone reflection. Nadia ordered for them from a restaurant she knew well, a regional favorite of Don Lucci's. If St. Louis had an unnamed sister city, the seaside promenade of Reggio di Calabria would be Kiener Plaza's better-looking twin. It looked like half of the Roman Coliseum, its stone benches descending into step-seats that opened to the Strait of Messina, its deep blue water fed from both the Mediterranean and Tyrrhenian Seas. They settled on the steps to enjoy grilled rolls of swordfish filled with parsley, pine nuts, parmesan and breading. The skyline was capped with a mixture of silent volcanic mountains and commercial and residential rises. The fact that it was reminiscent of Kiener back home in St. Louis, a

185

landmark for their romance and friendship, took Mia's breath away. The calming ballet of waves danced to the chorus of the breeze and strummed the shoreline, mesmerizing Ty and Mia as they stood captivated at the edge of the promenade overlooking the water, as Carlo and Nadia watched. Carlo finally interrupted their Hallmark moment, "Hey lovebirds, hate to break up your magic, but we have to move out before the weather storms in!" The plane was but a mile away so they bypassed the taxi to take in more of Reggio before departing. Although a certified pilot with the ratings to prove he could navigate the most tumultuous weather conditions, Carlo decided it would be best to stay grounded as the conditions worsened more quickly than projected. He always took extreme caution when traveling with passengers, and this was no exception. The storms wouldn't pass for three or four hours along the northern route that they would take to Rome, so Carlo altered his plans, calculating a 20-minute flight to Naples, then westward around the storm's eye. This would also allow Ty and Mia to taste Naples, yet another flavor of Italy. Boarding the plane as the gusts blew their bags wayward, "Buckle up!" Carlo called, and taxied quickly down the boutique runway to take off.

"Carlo, are you flying into the eye of the storm?" Nadia asked her brother. Her confidence in his aerial skills was bested only by her fear of thunderous weather. "Next stop…Napoli!" Carlo exclaimed, explaining his alternate travel plans of laying over in Naples for a few hours instead. It didn't matter to Ty and Mia, who wanted to embrace as much of Italy as they could, knowing that the weariness awaiting them when they returned home would be far worse than the physical tiredness of their travels. The mere thought of returning to the trials of life at home and giving up the freedom to be themselves here, weighed heavy as a dumbbell on Mia, as she nestled her head

186

on Ty's lap. They descended upon the rainy Naples skyline, guided by lights adorning the arched walkway overlooking the harbor. As they approached, Ty could see couples in intimately embraces watching the reflection of their landing lights twinkle across the water.

Italy's reputation as a haven for romantics was never more evident as it was in such warm displays of public affection. With only a few hours to spend on the ground, Carlo and Nadia took Ty and Mia to Rouge Napoli, a Neapolitan jazz and soul cabaret. The intimate joint generated an underground feel, lit only by candles atop the bistro tables. Janice Sing, a sultry, silken-voiced ex-pat who'd arrived in Naples from Harlem by way of St. Louis was the featured jazz performer. She was marketed as Italy's Lena Horne. Meeting fellow Americans so far from home created an immediate bond between Sing, Ty and Mia. Ty wasted no time asking the petite singer to begin her set with a request for his special friend. As he returned to his seat next to Mia, she met him with an inquisitive smile. "What?" he asked, grinning innocently. Carlo and Nadia grinned at their banter.

Sing wore a Billie Holiday flower tucked behind her ear, and a flowing, layered strapless dress that flared out at the bottom. "Good evening, I want to dedicate this song to my American compatriots, Mia and Ty, who are celebrating the first day of their forever," she said as she began… "*Innnnnseparable…that's how it ought to be, inseparable….*," easing into a rendition of Natalie Cole's classic that she nailed as if it were her own. The foursome enjoyed hours of music and drinks. Ty and Mia savored their last intimate moments of Italy before they departed for Rome's airport and Ty and Mia's flight back to the States. The weather had cleared enough for takeoff, but by the time they arrived on the tarmac in Rome, they had little time for good-byes. A shuttle met their private jet to transport them to their departing terminal.

"Ty, my brother, it's been a pleasure. You have the hand of the Luccis friendship, Carlo said, as he embraced Ty with a kiss on both cheeks. His words were drowned out by Mia and Nadia crying and

laughing as they hugged and vowed to see one another again soon.
Ty and Mia finally tore themselves away and were forced to check
their bags at the gate to avoid any delay. Boarding, they looked out
the terminal window, pausing to wave down to Carlo and Nadia
before settling in their first-class seats. The non-stop itinerary of
their trip had left them utterly exhausted, but they were nevertheless
filled with joy beyond their wildest expectations. The eight-hour
journey would provide much needed rest for their bodies, but their
minds were both weighed down by the anxiety of what lay ahead
back home.

CHAPTER XX

The Unseen Hand

Seven days had passed since Ty and Mia left St. Louis for Tivoli, under everyone's radar but Ms. Whitmore's. Tipped off by Pam, Bri was consumed with a need for unbridled revenge. Never before had Bri felt completely powerless over Mia. A hustler by nature, Bri had given himself over completely to the ruthless pursuit of power. Big Red's protection had been his for years, along with access to a reach that stretched into the media, the courts, prosecutors, police, prisons and loyal street muscle – muscle that began to atrophy under the Bri's direction. Big Red still oversaw the hustle, while Bri paid a hefty percentage to Red's organization for that reach.

Big Red's prison operation centered at the Big Sandy Penitentiary in Inez, Kentucky, where he was reputed to be part of the supreme council of the BGF (Black Guerilla Family) that ran the inside as well as the streets. Red's legions of support flowed into tributaries throughout the prison system, from Marion, Forrest City, Yazoo and Leavenworth penitentiaries. His influence with the BGF underwrote and secured his interests in the streets. Big Red had grown weary of his understudy's poor handling of his own personal and business matters, as they began to reflect on the organization. Red's lack of confidence in Bri was exacerbated by rumors of Bri's involvement with his daughter, Pam, which was expressly forbidden, and her growing drug indulgences, primarily compliments of Bri. Big Red finally summoned Bri to his council at Big Sandy. Big Red was also

190

Mia's adopted godfather, and he'd always viewed her as a positive and balancing force in Pam's life. Mia was naturally taken with Big Red and his paternal affection in the absence of her father.

In spite of his criminal indiscretions, Big Red was a man who devoutly espoused family values, loyalty and respect for women and the elderly. And he expected the same, without compromise, from his underlings and associates. Bri sat in his office in paranoid silence, broken intermittently by the annoying ringing of the phone. "Dammit!" Bri said, frustrated, noticing the call came from a correctional facility. He was all too familiar with the jailhouse recording from his own stint in the pen.

"This call originates from a correctional facility, this call is being monitored…" Bri picked up as the recording continued to play. "This call is from…Red Wright…a prisoner at a federal correctional facility," the recording continued.

With a sigh of anxiety, he pressed five to accept the call. "Brandon, I'm starting to feel unloved. I heard you threw a party with a big crowd but they left early!" came Big Red's calm baritone, spelling out Bri's transgressions in code. Red heard whispers of Bri shortchanging people on the street – screwing a loyal customer base built by 40 years of generosity and square dealing. Big Red had carved out a niche for Bri in the heroin market, just enough to buoy his fledgling club and his gambling exploits. Clearing his throat, Bri responded, "Yes sir, the lights had been unplugged from the inside. I've been trying to find the short," in the coded language he knew Red would understand. Bri's explanation was that someone within the organization was siphoning money from the operation, due to no incompetence of his own. He wasn't about to admit that his focus had been blurred by Mia's absence and his own overindulgence in

191

blow was cutting into profits. "In about two weeks…" Bri started, but not before he unwittingly revealed something of a business nature.

"Hey, young blood, it would be good to see you soon. Time is about to expire, gotta go…God be with you," Big Red said, sounding every bit the reformed inmate #15552-044. But Bri understood what the COs who monitored the calls didn't. Big Red was angry, and his subtle suggestions were clear commands that if not followed would be handled with extreme prejudice. Bri knew he had to pay a personal visit soon to discuss what was bothering Red. His mind raced around endless tracks of paranoid fear.

Did Red know about his past history with Pam? Is he going to take the rap for Pam's downward spiral? Did Red get word that the Feds were on to Bri? These questions ran through his head, scrambling his senses like an egg. The latter would certainly bring the wrath of Big Red's muscle; Red had warned his people to stay low-key in light of his pending appeal. The appellate judge had ordered a re-trial because of prosecutorial misconduct. He knew that the feds and attorney general would use any tie to an outside criminal enterprise to improve their weak case.

The week prior to his planned visit to Red, Bri had become but a shell of his once confident self, growing increasingly bitter at his inability to break through the ceiling of the Midwest's crime hierarchy. He hated feeling relegated to being Big Red's boy, especially when, by all appearances, he had no other way to make a move up. For Big Red, Bri had never posed, to any traceable degree, a threat. Red saw Bri as a weak hand with a strong mack – fine qualities for a pimp, but not for a strong head or organizational boss. It was this very notion that made Bri dangerous – his instability, fear, jealousy and nothing more problematic than his insatiable desire to be on top. Bri was smart enough to know that these things could never rear their ugly heads. He knew Big Red would be quick to end it all.

With his street muscle and political, media and judicial connections, Big Red could cut people a hundred ways before they even knew they were bleeding…Bri was unsettled, unable to gauge the root of Big Red's anger. He kept calm with steady infusions of Oxycotin, cocaine and alcohol. It gave him a misguided and self-deluded rise of a ruthless pressure valve within. Bri's growing agitation with the lack of respect he thought was due him from Big Red, secretly harboring dreams of toppling the boss. In his mind, he'd already struck an indirect blow by how he was handling Red's daughter, Pam. Pam, blinded by her desire for Bri and self-esteem so low that Bri could control it remotely, took whatever mental, psychological and physical abuse he meted out. She rationalized this mistreatment as a part of the game she had to endure, like young college girl trying to survive the hazing so she could join a coveted sorority.

Bri traveled the 300 miles to Inez, Kentucky where Big Sandy Penitentiary was located. The entire trip, he conjured up a variety of excuses to meet Big Red's possible concerns. The barbed wire surrounding the pen had a sobering effect on Bri, forcing him to consider the potential fallout from people he had messed over along the way.

Entering the facility, Bri was met by scanners and prison guards, inquiring about who he was there to see. "Reginaldo Wright, #15552-044," Bri informed the guard.

"Oh, Big Red? Ah ite….hold a minute," the burly officer said, as he consorted with another supervising officer on duty. Big Red was no ordinary inmate, as he'd curried favor with the prison officials. His visits rarely followed normal procedures, as he was afforded private space apart from the visiting room and common areas. "This way!" The guard said, escorting Bri to a private room, sheltered from view by tinted windows.

Big Red sat in a high-back leather chair facing the door, as if it was his own office. He was dressed in his prison-issued green uniform, creased with military precision, and shoes that shined like Windex on patent leather. "Brandon. How are you, Young Blood?" Big Red greeted him, arms extended in welcome. Big Red used formal names in public discourse, so as to not legitimize in any way the street stigmas that seemed to follow them.

"Good to see you Mr. Wright. I'm good, and I see time has been good to you as well," Bri responded with a nervous smile. The guard knocked once on the door to signal that the microphones were disconnected, allowing them to talk business without monitoring.

"I'm not pleased at some of the things that I'm hearing!" Big Red stated. "The first rule when you're stuck in a hole is to stop digging!" Red added, his words wrapped in disappointment. "The club is upside down, people ain't gettin' paid and you haven't put a dent in the 300 large!" Big Red continued, his voice rising with frustration. "Now, I got my appeal comin' up. I need you to add five to that three and thank the judge in advance for me. You dig, Young Blood?" Big Red finished, scaling back to calm.

 Red had worked a deal through a friend of his, appellate judge, Hank Yateru, who was hearing his case, for a favorable ruling of release. Bri knew that Big Red would take any hesitation as a refusal, as disrespect and inaptitude, all of which would be met with an undesirable fate. Bri sat silently, looking Big Red directly in the eyes and nodding, careful not to give away the impossibility of the task set before him. Big Red's life and freedom depended on him. "Say no more, Big Red…it's done!" Bri assured him, emphatically.

"Good, good!" Big Red nodded, placing his hand firmly on Bri's shoulder as if to instill confidence and convey the severe consequences of failure.

After an awkward moment of silence, Bri bowed his head in almost shameful humility, "Big, I need the favor of your hand?" he asked. Big Red had already extended his hand many times, bailing out Bri's cash-strapped operation with an infusion of hundreds of thousands of dollars, and the guarded hand of his relationships. Red's long silence and straight-laced, expressionless face unnerved Bri.

"What is it, Young Blood?" Red asked.

"I have a little tumor that I need surgically removed and I believe my body would be a lot healthier," Bri answered. "I just need to confer with proper staff to make sure the scar heals right," Bri added, speaking in coded language. Big Red understood. There was a problem standing in the way, he presumed of business that needed to be taken care of methodically through the use of Big Red's network.

"God, I'M TIRED OF THIS JOKER," Red sighed to himself. But he knew that if he helped Bri get his business bearings, Bri could deliver on his debt. "Ah ite, Young Blood, you got it, now get it together. I don't like looking bad!" Red said. Raising his brow,

195

touching his finger to the table with exclamatory question, "It's surgical, right?" Red asked pointedly.

"Yes sir, it won't spread!" Bri answered, understanding that this generous gesture was specific only to the immediate problem.

"Ah ite, you got it, any flare-ups after this, I suggest you self-medicate!" Big Red made his point.

"Understood!" Bri said, fighting to hold his smile in.

"By the way, how is that lovely wife of yours?" Red asked of Bri.

"Fine, Big, fine. Thanks for asking," Bri responded, wondering if the question was veiled. Big Red was oblivious to the identity of Bri's target, intentionally not seeking the info, avoiding any direct association. Red knew of Tyson Penn and respected his ability to maneuver through the various channels of business, politics and the streets without being consumed by it. He viewed this ability as the result of great fortitude and strength, an asset rare in one so young age. Big Red's generosity and his choice not to question Bri for specifics changed the game in ways they could not now fathom.

Leaving the prison, Bri felt new life breathed into him. He now had an arsenal at his disposal to bring down any foe without brandishing a weapon. This is what tempered anyone's ambition to try trumping Big Red's authority. He had emissaries of law and the courts on lock. With his operation centered strategically in the Gateway to the West, Red was the powerbroker of many transactions connecting the east and west coasts, even the waterways of the Mississippi, where Red maintained influence with the port authorities. Now, Bri believed he had the American Express of influence, the black card of power. Bri's arrogance would now know no bounds, his wrath no limit. Mia had become his obsession; he blamed her absence for his downward spiral. Her value had grown to an appreciable level in his heart, even as he seethed with rage. His lucid dreams of Mia and Ty together drove him to a near manic state of vengeance. Now, feeling comfortably in control, Bri rolled across I-64 listening to Bootsy Collins "I Rather Be with You" on repeat, dazed and unfazed by the haze of the smoke that clouded the Aston interior. "Yeah, my time. Day for orders is ova'!" he thought to himself, taking a lung-filling drag of smoke. Belting out the song's refrain…"Said I ratha be with you…."

CHAPTER XXI

The Set-up

District Attorney Franklin Stephenson had recently been narrowly elected over long-time incumbent, Jennifer James, a Caucasian woman popular among both whites and blacks in the highly polarized city. Her tenure had been plagued with a continuous string of murders and crime that placed St. Louis at the top in almost every statistical category for crime nationwide. She was a political anomaly, a well-liked, straight-shooting do-gooder who often found herself pitted against the police department, as their corruption forced the DA's office to drop most of its cases. Ty had been an ardent supporter and friend of James after they met on a community volunteer project during their senior year of high school. James' well-intentioned efforts to clean up the streets were crippling the criminal crock-pot from which the drug dealers, City Hall and the police department ate. Eventually, an undercurrent of negative national attention and the election of the first black president brought droves of the city's black youth to the polls and swept political neophyte Franklin Stephenson into office. Stephenson, a young, sharp-tongued, street-wise brother was new to the political arena, but an incumbent of the streets.

"I be damned...Lil' Frank!" Bri exclaimed, shouldering his way up to the new DA through the capacity crowd at Stephenson's victory party.

"Whatcha know, Bri?" Stephenson said.

"I wouldn't have believed it if I didn't see it with my own eyes," Bri laughed. "Congratulations!" he toasted the new DA and his old juvenile cellmate. Lil Frank had spent a year in juvenile for a string of car thefts and an assault while working with Bri. Both were brought up under the street tutelage of Big Red, a visionary who planned to have a perpetual power base and influence that wouldn't come by happenstance.

Big Red strategically groomed each person in a specific area, paying for their education and training - law schools, police academies, labor unions, journalists, etc. In addition to these vested interests, he had his ground crew, their lieutenants and capos. This set-up was constructed as protective insulation for expanding his empire, solidifying the future of his crime family. Lil' Frank was one of the few whose chosen career path was law. In spite of his juvenile criminal indiscretions, Lil Frank was an intelligent, stand-up kid who'd ingratiated himself to Red with his calm demeanor and a knack for understanding the law. Under Big Red's guidance, he completed his GED, graduated from Texas Southern and received his law degree from the Thurgood Marshall School of Law. Bri, who preceded Lil Frank out of Red's stable, had made his name in the club and adult entertainment industry. Bri had been tasked by Big Red to take care of any of his "little brother's" expenses, which effectively kept prospects an arm's length away from Big Red. Bri knew now why Red placed an emphasis on attending the victory party. It put him square in the midst of the players he needed to solve his problem. Across the room at the bar, an elegant sister locked eyes with Bri and he could see her trying to figure out how she knew him. He was never one to forget a name or face, a character trait central to his street charm.

Making his way to the bar, "Hello, I couldn't help but notice…" Bri started.

"Yes, Marion Evans. How are you, Brandon?" she said.

"Wow! Time must be standin' still in your world. You're as stunning as you were when I was…"

"A little snotty-nose charmer, "she said smiling.

"My nose don't run no more," Bri chuckled.

"I see!" Ms. Evans responded. Marion Evans had been a sitter for Big Red's wife, and later ran a not-for-profit boys' youth organization.

Red helped to orchestrate the funding of UpArch, a program that worked in conjunction with the juvenile courts as the next step in their probationary period. Marion had ascended to the federal bench via an appointment by Senator Clay Evers. The seat had been vacated by Judge Autrel'H.G.' Smith, when embarrassing allegations of him sodomizing a group of male law clerks were made public. Bri knew with a certainty that Big Red, in his role as the unseen hand of the Midwest, had figured into the ascent of Ms. Evans to the judgeship.

Unknown, though, was that Big Red had given her the green light on Bri. As the crowd silenced, "We will fight crime in the streets, City Hall or whoever, whenever and wherever it rears its ugly head…Not by my will, but the will of the people!" roared the newly elected district attorney, closing his victory speech that was met with thunderous applause. Bri smiled, laughing inwardly as his belief that politicians and preachers were all hypocrites was affirmed.

"Here's a crook who's protecting and working for crooks," he thought. He understood that the law occasionally cast its net over low- and mid-level crime elements to satisfy the public's outcry for action, and of course for their self-serving pursuits of higher office. It didn't matter, so long as it worked for him.

Nor did DA Stephenson and Judge Evans climb to their respective ranks by being oblivious to one hand washing the other, especially the hand that stirred their pots of success. "Life is good," was their cue that the word came down from Red and he'd sanctioned further conversations.

The crowded public event was ideal. No one could claim they'd orchestrated something that stemmed from a chance meeting between the three. Bri, Judge Evans and DA Stephenson inconspicuously left the crowd for a brief meeting in a private room atop the Coronado building. Bri wasted no time. "I have a thorn that needs a vacation in a controlled environment. I believe it will serve us all in our efforts to fight the ugly head of crime," Bri's smirk mocked the speech of the district attorney. Being able to use the very vehicles that Big Red helped to create was an honor, and. The idea of a high profile case from some well-respected, unsuspecting mark was just the PR the new District Attorney and Judge could use for an immediate career boost.

"Who?" Stephenson asked.

"I'll let you know once I've finalized the other pieces. I have a few loose ends to tie up," Bri said, shaking his head, smiling as he turned for the door. "Man, how far we have come!

Congratulations again, family…One!" Bri now needed only specific bait and to determine the how and where they would bring it all to the fore. He knew Ty was smart and savvy and that if he didn't act quickly, the full, misguided bulk of Bri's plan would be revealed, which would cause Big Red to pull his support and put many others at a professional risk.

Ty and Mia's Return

"We'll begin our descent into St. Louis in approximately 15 minutes. Skies are slightly overcast and the temperature is a pleasant 72 degrees," the captain announced. As Flight 1217 descended past the St. Louis Arch, Ty and Mia grasped hold of one another, their eyes spoke volumes about the reality of what lay ahead once they landed. Ty began prepping Mia for their plan upon arrival, which started with exiting the plane separately. Mia was instructed to go immediately to the baggage claim and proceed to a pre-arranged taxi service. They knew they must not be romantically linked, not now. Even though Mia and Bri were separated, they were still married, and certain aspects of their marriage contract would be rendered void by a divorce due to infidelity. Mia might have to assume civil liability for too much of Bri's mess. Ty was aware that he could bear the brunt of the financial burden if that were so.

For Mia, who had become accustomed to being at Ty's side over the past few days, even the thought of a ride in separate taxis caused minor separation anxiety. Nevertheless, the clicking of seatbelts and shuffling passengers told them they had to disembark. Mia made her way off the plane quickly and Ty waited for every other passenger to depart. She embraced him before she left, her kiss no less desperate than if she were sending him to the front lines in Afghanistan. As their lips parted, Ty smiled at her, "What was that for?" Ty asked, staring deeply enough into her eyes to see his own reflection in her pupils.

"Just because," she murmured, copying Ty's own unconditional expression of love, one he'd lifted from Anita Baker's song of the same name.

After all the passengers were offloaded and the arrival gate emptied, Ty headed for the baggage carousel, knowing his luggage would be the lone bag or placed in the baggage claim office. When he saw the empty carousel, he headed for the claim office. "Tyson Penn, American Flight 1217," he told the attendant. Looking over the bags, Ty pointed his out.

"Here you go," she lifted it over the counter.

"Thank you, Ma'am," Ty answered, and made his way to the passenger pick-up where his black Lincoln taxi waited. A baggage handler ran dutifully towards Ty to assist him with his luggage when he exited the terminal. After the courteous gentleman situated his bag in the trunk, Ty slipped him a tip and, exhausted from the trip and the wrangling, he threw his head back on the seat and closed his eyes.

Awakening almost immediately to the sounds of hard braking and doors shutting, Ty jerked forward as the taxi came to a screeching halt just as soon as it took off. Two unmarked white Chevy Malibus positioned themselves in front of and behind Ty's taxi. "Driver, keep your hands on the steering wheel...You, in the rear, hands out the window... slowly open the door and place your hands over your head!" the detective instructed Ty and the driver with his pistol drawn.

Ty calmly heeded every instruction. "What's going on?" he asked.

"FBI! Tyson Penn?" the agent asked, one hand resting on the pistol and the other showing identification. Puzzled, Ty maintained outward calm by focusing on minor details. "Damn dirty shoe mutha@#%...." he thought to himself, lamenting the agents as unkempt slouches who neglected the cleanliness of their shoes.

As the TSA and DEA officials arrived, Ty was escorted into one of their vehicles. Ty watched helplessly, handcuffed in the backseat, as the four officials removed and rummaged through his suit and briefcases. "Bingo!" the DEA agent said, pulling two packages of what appeared to be cocaine and a pistol from his luggage.

"Hey, come look at this?" FBI Agent Moreno called to the TSA officer. "Whattaya make of this?" he asked.

"Wow. Looks like a schematic drawing of the terminals and duct systems of the airport," the officer answered, looking over papers apparently pulled from Ty's briefcase.

Agent Moreno approached the vehicle, "Tyson Sheldon Penn, you're under arrest!" He proceeded to read him his Miranda rights before immediately transporting him to a secured location, where Ty was booked. Once the agents arrived, Ty was seated at a lone table in a wooden chair. Agent Moreno slid a tape recorder in front of him, hoping to capture some admission of guilt. Ty, the ever-astute attorney, exercised his right to silence, refusing to cave to their intense questioning.

"PROMINENT ATTORNEY BUSTED," read the headlines of the St. Louis Patriot, a weekly African-American publication controlled by white interests but ingratiated to Big Red. The paper's editor was an arrogant Caucasian named Jake King, whose strange mix of liberal leaning and racist superiority was given minor credibility in the black weekly. He took pleasure in blacklisting powerful, successful free-thinking black men, especially a young one like Ty. Ty's popularity and position hadn't been anointed by the power structure or validated by the black bourgeoisie. Although the Patriot's masthead screamed its motto of expanding and representing the interests of the black community, it merely sought to control the political and social agenda of the city. It had become the token that protected a sheep-like status quo of black political, social and economic inferiority and the impotence of the masses.

Ty read the headline, wondering to himself how such a paper could continuously attack blacks without the community seeing through it. It had never been Ty's style to kiss anyone's proverbial ring, especially one so obviously seeking to be the conduit of power. He paid respect to those worthy of respect. Many admired his earthy, proletariat-leaning, humble style, just as many envied what they lacked the courage to be…genuine, fearless and socially conscious. The Patriot became the vehicle that would poison the public well against Ty, per the hidden sanction of Big Red Wright. Weekly articles and commentaries attacked his credibility and chipped away at his popularity. Ty drew the ire of the editor by refusing to respond to the personal attacks or interview requests - an affront the editor did not appreciate. Ty himself didn't care about the negative press, except for the impact it had on his family, and of course, on Mia. She was bombarded by stories and lies that contradicted all that she'd come to believe of Ty. She believed none of it, she knew for certain that she loved Ty and she was torn only by her helplessness to fix anything.

Locked Down

Ty pleaded his innocence to Mia while confined in a holdover cell awaiting a bond hearing. The impenetrable Plexiglas separated Ty and his high-powered defense attorney, Pauly D'Amato at the St. Louis County Jail. This was unusually difficult for Pauly who spent much time at the detention facility defending cases, and making legal visits to clients. But this was different. This was a friend to whom he'd been close since junior high. "Hey man, how you holding up T.?" Pauly asked.

Somber and still riddled with disbelief, "Man, I, I..., I didn't do it, whatever they say it is!" Ty said struggling to find the words. "It's a set- up, Pauly, you know it's not my m.o.," he added.

"I believe you, bro. But it's making a judge and jury believe that we gotta worry about. It isn't getting' any easier with the media clawin' you deep already," Pauly said with a frown.

"What are we looking at?" Ty asked.

"I'm in the dark, I don't know the charges yet, but they say it's four counts," said Pauly.

"What?" Ty exclaimed.

"Let's just see what we're working with. We'll meet downturn in about forty-eight hours to negotiate a plea or fight," Pauly nodded, his smile aimed at relaxing Ty. It was a common prosecutorial maneuver to stack charges, no matter how far out they might be, then negotiate down to the primary charges they want to stick. The current climate of public mistrust in politics and the legal sectors, this would likely not be a trial of guilt or innocence but of prevailing public sentiment. Ty, being an astute attorney, understood the choices given by the Feds and prosecutors are never real choice at all. Nevertheless, he was prepared to meet with the Feds and prosecutor and see what they offered him before they issued a formal indictment. As he left, Pauly tried to sound reassuring. "If you need anything else, let me know," he told Ty.

"Thanks man!" Ty said as he turned away, then quickly turned back. "Hey Pauly, would you contact Mia for me? Let her know I'm OK, that I'm innocent…and 1-4-3," he added.

"1-4-3?" Pauly asked.

"She'll understand." Ty told him, sparing Pauly an inconsequential explanation. Ty then handed him a letter via the guard to give Mia. The numbers 1-4-3 was a code they'd used to say "I love you," each number corresponding to the number of letters in the word.

"Alright man, will do!" Pauly bumped Ty's fist against the glass, while the guard hovered, indicating time was up. Pauly and Ty knew the system well enough – if you ran crosshairs with the Feds, the least they'd do is draw blood, if they didn't severe your head altogether.

Ty sat in his cell, watching the other inmates play dominoes and chess. He resolved not to accustom himself to the leisure activity of incarceration. Lying atop his bunk, staring at the cracking paint on the ceiling, he wondered exactly who and what was at the root of this. Ty had never crossed anyone. He was a straight-shooting businessman well-regarded for his integrity. He could only surmise jealousy as a motive.

At that instant, Ty knew, at his very core, that it was Bri. Furious at his own naiveté for not realizing it from jump, he pounded the bunk. The incident at the club, the attempt on his life – Bri must at least suspect the extent of his relationship with Mia, enough to sharpen the diabolical claws of the man's unbridled wrath and envy.

Monday morning, Pauly was at DA Stephenson's office door when he arrived to review the evidence. He had to gauge Ty's defensibility and determine an appropriate plea. "Good morning, sir, and belated congratulations on your victory." Pauly extended his hand to the newly elected DA.

"Thank you," Stephenson responded, all business.

"I should hope to extend such good fortune into my client's case," Pauly said light-heartedly to relax the initial meeting, which drew a chuckle from the DA.

Pauly, although one of the higher profile defense attorneys, was serious by nature, with a Perry Mason-style approach to legal proceedings. He was well-liked among many prosecutors, judges and fellow lawyers for his pleasant disposition and thorough defense preparation. He began viewing the file that the DA handed him, with pictures of Ty in the company of Romel, meeting with club owners, and reputed Houston drug kingpin Kai Banks. The second was a picture with Abdullah Khan, a Palestinian immigrant with alleged ties to Hamas, who evidently was an FBI informant, turned after being threatened with deportation for money laundering and welfare fraud. "Ok, so what's the tie? Pictures? Of what?" Pauly quizzed with photos in hand, closing the folder and sliding it across the table as if nothing was there.

"A briefcase, thumbprints, engraved with the letters T-S-P (Tyson Sheldon Penn) holding three kilos of cocaine, a .45 caliber pistol and a map of airport schematics," DA Stephenson responded with the confidence of a man who believed he could make it all connect. "Conspiracy, possession with intent and a witness who says he's part of an elaborate scheme to funnel money to Hamas through drug sales, along with conspiracy to commit a terrorist act!" Stephenson summed up the charges triumphantly.

Pauly's cool demeanor never thawed. He leaned back in his chair as the magnitude of what his longtime friend faced set in. "DA, I know this guy, I'll put my life on it that he's not good for this. Where the hell is this coming from?" he asked quietly. His question was met with silence. The DA gazed out the window, smiling inwardly. Pauly sensed the DA wouldn't budge.

"Fifteen on the drugs, five for the gun, 25 to life on the conspiracy," Stephenson said. "But I know you, Pauly; you'll use every legal maneuver you've got to fight this, and not the city or your client can bear the cost of a protracted legal battle." he added. "Plead to conspiracy on the drug charge, and I'll get your fifteen to five on money laundering. After that, I can't be responsible for the prejudiced wrath of a lily white jury," the DA offered.

Pauly stood up to make his way toward the door, "Give me a few days to consult with my client," Pauly answered.

"You've got 24 hours." the DA dismissed him with a cocky nod toward the door.

Pauly understood the legal system well enough to know that actual innocence or guilt is often immaterial. What matters is what you can prove or disprove, along with what kind of public sentiment might have colored potential jurors.

America's phobia of terror was imbedded so deeply in the country's psyche after 9/11 that even alleging terrorism was the surest way to prejudice the pool. Leaving the district attorney's office, Pauly immediately headed to see Ty at the jail. The queasy feeling intensified in his belly with every step toward his friend, as he tried to make sense of what seemed to be the inevitable…Ty facing serious jail time.

Ty and Pauly wanted to get past this as quickly as possible, but they weren't the only ones operating on a timeline. DA Stephenson and Judge Evans couldn't afford Ty not accepting a plea deal. Fighting the case in open court risked the possibility of exposing judicial and prosecutorial impropriety, and if a connection to Bri could be established, serious damage to Big Red.

In the visiting room, the anxiety was thick on both sides of the glass as Ty and Pauly sat and picked up the phones. Pauly mustered a smile that hid his feeling of helplessness to turn things in Ty's favor. Ty had put on that same smile for enough clients to read through it instantly, and his face wore the exhaustion of a defeated general. "Listen, give it to me straight!" Ty commanded Pauly.

Pauly laid out the details of the evidence presented from the DA's office. Ty interrupting him, "What the hell?! What brief case and what pistol? Do I look like a dope-pushing Bin Laden?" Ty seethed, angrily pounding the table and drawing the guard's attention.

"Easy Ty, I'm on your side," Pauly said, trying to calm him.

"It's obvious someone has the fix in!" Ty exclaimed.

"My job is to defend you and I'll put everything I have into it. Whether it's a fix or not, it's thick and we've gotta make some tough decisions," Pauly said. "Life without and 25 is a death sentence, Pauly, I can't lay down on that!" Ty shook his head.

"Ok, then, brotha' - let's get ready to rumble!" Pauly smiled, fist bumping Ty through the glass. To assure Ty of his commitment, Pauly called the DA's office in his presence. "DA Stephenson? This is D'Amato. We won't need those 24 hours. We'll see you in court!" Pauly exacted the same cockiness he'd received from Stephenson earlier. Stephenson held the phone, speechless, before he slowly hung up. He'd gone from being sure he'd slam-dunked the scare tactics to feeling his bluff had just been called.

After repeated plea offerings from the DA's office were met by Ty's consistent refusal to accept them, the indictment went forward despite severe reservations on the part of the judge and DA. Bri could almost taste the fruits of his medley of deceptive plots. He toiled to hide his immense pleasure at watching the beginning of the end for Ty. Knowing that he might fall under a cloud of suspicion, Bri sought to cover any hints of his involvement.

He put the word out that he was angry about Ty's arrest and that he wanted information about anyone's involvement. He adamantly claimed Ty's innocence in his inner circles. "Ty's a good dude, man, he helped me...he helped us! I want the motherfucka responsible for this!" Bri yelled theatrically, slamming his fist on the table upstairs at Movado where his closest associates gathered.

They noted what a departure this was from the night of Mia's fortieth birthday party when the tensions between Ty and Bri had escalated to Cold War levels. But Bri was well aware of the fondness his own inner circle felt for Ty. He knew that if he was suspected in any way, his ranks could divide and crumble. Even though this action had been sanctioned by Big Red, it remained a covert, renegade move that had exceeded the scope of what was permitted because it had nothing to do with business beyond the $250K debt to Ty on which Bri sought to renege, unbeknownst to Big Red and his crew. Bri had dug his hole so deep that only his cocaine-fueled delusions of grandeur could occasionally lift him from the reality of his failures. There was still the issue of the $500K he had to make good on to obtain Big Red's release from prison. Bri's business and personal affairs were on the brink of implosion with him growing more desperate as his plans struggled to unfold.

Bri had no one to bring into his misguided actions because he couldn't trust revealing his bigger, underlying intentions. He longed to talk with Mia, but was careful not to overreach, knowing that the situation with Ty had her unnerved, which would only get worse if he contacted her now.

He hoped to curry favor with Mia through a gallant offer of help. Bri thought this would make him look good while throwing a red herring to distract her from seeing his involvement and boiling rage. Getting Ty out of the way would ease open the door to Mia on top of exacting revenge. Bri turned first to Pam to gauge where Mia was emotionally, letting her act as messenger for his generous overtures of assistance. Pam's intensifying addiction, spawned by her illusions of being Bri's woman, left her an indentured servant to meet his every request. He waited outside the nail shop Pam frequented. He paid for her standing weekly appointment, one more of his investments on which she depended. Waiting for her nails to dry, Pam followed the stares of the shop's other patrons who had fixated on the steel blue Aston-Martin parking out front. With her nails barely dry, Pam hopped up, quickly gathering her purse. Chewing incessantly on a piece of gum that seemed to have lost its elasticity, Pam approached the car. The tinted window lowered and Minnie Riperton's *"Come Inside Me"* blasted through the speakers as a mellowed Bri gazed over his oversized Prada shades, "let's ride!" he said.

Reclined back in her seat, Pam playfully reached for Bri's knee, but he intercepted her hand. "Business before pleasure," he chided.

"OK, Daddy. What's up?"

After the song's end, he asked if she'd talked to Mia.

"No!" Pam answered, her tone tinged with jealousy.

Bri grabbed a palm full of hair from the back of her head. "Look! Don't get the game twisted. Check it!" Bri said, removing his shades, to make sure she understood how serious he was.

"Ah ite. OK, baby, I'm sorry, please!" Pam lowered her voice to a more humble and submissive octave.

He loosened his grip. "I need you to reconnect. Regain her confidence. Let her know you heard I want to pay for his legal defense," Bri instructed Pam.

If there were degrees in gossip, Pam would have achieved her

CMG (Certified Master Gossiper). Although her stories were met by many with kind of the skepticism they saved for National Enquirer, her stories did contain kernels of believability. She dropped her seeds of bad information, and Bri harvested their negative yield. With Ty out of the way, Mia could be easily rendered vulnerable to well-veiled schemes hidden in the comforting overtures of associates and so-called friends.

Bri circled back around to the nail shop where Pam's car was parked. "We cool?" Bri asked.

"I got it!" Pam affirmed. She dutifully completed the orders she received from Bri, anticipating a treat like an obedient dog from his master. She believed her reward was always a bigger piece of Bri, her drug-addled brain incapable of seeing how he used her.

Pam was well aware of Mia's Saturday morning ritual excursion to the Soulard Farmer's Market. She'd lose herself in the crowds and buy her fruits and vegetables for the week, finding solace away from her busy, stressful life. Pam staked out a spot near one of the flower vendors where she could watch for Mia in the hopes of sinking the venomous fangs of her friendship back into Mia.

Saturday morning greeted Mia curled up on her chaise lounge after a restless, lonely night. She rubbed her eyes and stretched to her feet, planning to get dressed and head to the market, when a news report about the accusations and charges against Ty played across her TV screen. She flipped the set off, slouching back into a heartbroken funk on the couch when the phone startled her. Unable to identify the number, she hesitated, finally picking up. "Hello?"

"Hi, Mia, this is Paul D'Amato, Tyson's attorney and friend."

"Yes!" Mia said, her heart picking up speed.

"Well, he wanted me to tell you that he's fine and that he's innocent, and, oh yes…1-4-3. He said you'd understand," Pauly said gently. Mia paused, covering her mouth as she fought back the tears. "Mia, we're gonna do everything we can, I promise. Just be strong," Pauly consoled her.

"Thank you. Tell him 1-4-3." Her voice grew stronger as she brushed the tears away.

"Will do - I'll keep you posted," Pauly assured her. The call injected Mia with enough energy to shake herself awake and head to the market. Normal routine would be good, she told herself. Relaxing. Picking through the vegetables and spices, Mia found peace in the vibrant, diverse energy of the market. She felt stronger, and a distance from her troubles, until Pam bumped into her as she paid for a box of strawberries.

Feigning surprise, Pam greeted her old friend. "Heyyy, girl?" How you doin'?" Pam asked.

Mia took a deep breath before she answered. "Girl, I wouldn't even know where to start, but I'm fine," she said, straightening her shoulders.

"I'm sorry to hear about Ty. I know what he means to you," Pam offered.

Shrugging, Mia shook her head lightly, "Thanks, Pam, but I'm sure he'll be OK," Mia was convincing herself more than Pam. She walked toward a bench outside the market, and without invitation, Pam sat down with her.

Continuing with unsolicited gossip, Pam lowered her voice. "Yeah, girl, I heard Bri was livid and wants to help pay for his defense," Mia sat stoically, refusing to run with Pam's conversational ball. She shared nothing with Pam, gave no information about herself or about Ty. Picking up on her vibe, Pam pulled back and excused herself. "I'm still here if you need me," she said, as she headed toward the street.

"Thanks, We'll talk sometime." Mia left it open, remembering Ty's warning before they'd traveled.

CHAPTER XXII

Judgment Day

As the crowd gathered outside Judge Yateru's courtroom on the fourteenth floor of the Justice Center, Mia's spirit filled the room. Even though she couldn't be there with him, her absence was nearly as powerful as her presence. Before court commenced, Ty stood in the atrium, staring out at a panoramic view of the downtown landscape, the stadium, the Arch, the Old Courthouse and Kiener Plaza, remembering and wondering if this scenic view would be his last. The potential permanency jarred him as Mia smiled at him from his mind's eye, and he knew he'd give up all the views in the world if he could keep from losing her. Ty knew that she sat somewhere nearby, but longed for her here, next to him, as he prepared to face his future.

Pauly had given him his phone, but he hesitated. He wasn't sure if contacting her would hurt more than not, and he didn't want to burden her either. Even as he tried holding on to optimism, his more realistic self had begun the process of "jailing," mentally forcing himself to prepare for the worst case scenario, distancing and hardening himself to the real possibility of prison. Ty knew the system, and he knew how easily one could err in administering justice. He understood the subjectivity of judges, often hidden behind the moniker of "blind justice." But he thought of Mia and could longer resist what might be a last opportunity to correspond with her normally. He drew strength from the love he tried to hold, and the way her face lit up for his affectionate overtures, none ever too small. Even as he began to text, he logged a smile, and for just a moment, relaxed, for the first time in weeks.

He sent his Mia a poem he'd written for as he'd waited in his cell at county. He'd written it in halting Italian, because he knew she'd understand how much he'd come to cherish her native tongue.

Mi Caro Mia Farone:

Isola Di Passione

Il fluso cosi uno fuime supra il rosso legnos

su il valle.

Portare prossimo rugiada.

Per nessuno prevederes il tuo belleza

Piu che io.

Nessuno viaggiare il profondia

Oppure coraggioso il stagione variare.

Il mio montagna cema dentro il sargentes acqua

di il valle.

Cosi io torre montare.

Fare irruzione il terra alto piano

Venire il Isola di Passione.

"Just in case my Midwestern country accent butchered your mother tongue, I will translate." Ty joked, then sent the same thing in English.

My Dear Mia Farone:

Isle of Passion

I flow as a river over the redwoods

Upon the valley

Brings forth dew.

For none foresees your beauty

more than I.

None travels the depth

or braves the season variance.

My mountain peaks into the spring water

of the valley.

As I tower erect,

breaking the earth's plateau;

Comes the Isle of Passion.

Ty smiled as he hit 'send.' Pauly, consorting with his co-counsel, glanced over at Ty and wondered in amazement how a man could find a moment of joy facing challenge before him. Ty took solace knowing that his words could paint a picture love for Mia, creating a deeper connection and holding them together. Just knowing that wherever Mia sat, she might be smiling at the same picture he'd painted for her with his words. That connection seemed to restore the blood flow to his soul.

Mia, as Ty guessed, sat in her car near the spot they'd first shared their desires at Kiener Plaza. Leaning back in her car, she was caught in a medley of tears and laughter, Mia listened to a CD that Ty had made her of songs connected to the experiences and conversations they'd shared.

As one Ty's favorites started, "You Don't Even Know" by Gerald Albright, Mia texted back: *"For every moment without chance or risk, is life lost. I've lived a thousand lives and moments of pure earthly ecstasy with you, all else is and was but seconds of time. You've re-routed the direction of the flow of my heart and it will travel with you to the end of the earth, till the end of time." love your Mia Flower*. She pressed send as the salty tears fell upon her phone like misty dew.

She hoped he understood her message, that he'd given her the freedom to feel absolute and complete without the weight of the world's opinion. She felt helpless to lift him from his legal situation, yet she empowered by the strength and depth of the love they shared. She had accomplished what, in her deep subconscious she'd set out to do when she finally left Bri...to free herself unto herself. And she'd been blessed with a love pure as an artesian spring and permanent as the Rock of Gibraltar in the process.

Some of Ty's associates had slowly distanced themselves from him and his case, but Mia had never considered leaving his side. No negative media account or public perception could counter what she knew of Ty, what she loved of Ty.

At that moment, her heart filled with a resolve to love him more. To love him openly. She realized that Bri could sue them both for spousal alienation once proof of infidelity was established. This had become a more common legal maneuver in cases of separation and divorce and it was not beyond him to exercise it as a monetary way to exact revenge and send a message. But Mia was no longer sure she cared.

Ty made his way into the packed court room. He had no tears to shed, only a cold numbness, built upon the public scorn and the many personal losses he'd endured over the years. Compared to the losses of family, this challenge couldn't rattle Ty. Facing probable jail time, he remained uncommonly calm.

Even with the thought that Mia could be exposed to more of Bri's evil and the wiles of men who had waited in the wings for his downfall, Ty had humbly resigned himself to the fact that his predicament had rendered him powerless, left with only the hope that God and their love would sustain and protect Mia.

District Attorney Stephenson was like an overconfident boxer looking to end a fight early, only to see it extend beyond his expectations. The public sentiment had already begun to marginally shift against the district attorney's office, fueled by rumors and half-stories and rumblings of impropriety, maybe even a conflict of interest between the DA and the judge.

If the case was prolonged any further, those few in the know feared that information could surface tying Bri and Big Red to the case, hampering any future political aspirations. The opportunity to fulfill their debts to Big Red via Bri couldn't have come soon enough. Getting this over, with the right verdict, would settle their world back firmly onto its axis.

Ty's family filled the front three rows, friends and associates had taken the back two rows, and Bri had tucked himself inconspicuously in the rear corner, out of direct view of the defendant's table. Ty knew in his soul that Bri must have had something to do with this. The time he'd spent in the holdover and every minute of quiet reflection since, had given him plenty of time to connect all the dots. His intuition was rarely wrong, a gift for which he was known.

Members of the media who had covered Ty's activities in the past, some of whom he had established good working relationships with, also sat in the courtroom, notepads in hand.

The FBI officials, even though they'd arrested him, seemed to like Ty, knowing with certainty that he was merely a pawn in someone else's game. They approached him and his attorney at their table. The agent had sat across from many a local politician and businessman who'd ran afoul of the law and would have sold their mothers to avoid the inside of a jail cell. There was a quiet resolve and strength about Ty that drew the female agent to him. "Hello, Ty," she greeted him, glancing down with remorse. Ty just smiled, offered a good-natured hello and warmly shook her hand.

DA Stephenson stood at the adjacent dais as Judge Evans called Ty and his attorney, Pauly D'Amato up.

And even in the midst of his trial, Ty refused to give those taking delight in his circumstances the benefit of seeing him stumble. He stood straight, strong and composed.

The judge called the jury foreman, and waited for her to make her way forward.

"In the case of the United States versus Tyson Sheldon Penn, we find the defendant guilty of conspiracy to trafficking, and possession of a firearm in prohibited Federal transit facility..." the foreman began. She went on, but Ty stood numb, his expressionless face hiding an inner conflict of rising anger and relief that at least the uncertainty was over. The thought of living in jail didn't hit Ty hardest. He was most devastated by yet another loss that his family would be forced to experience, his absence, the one they counted on most of all. And then Mia, left incarcerated in her own cell of loneliness.

The picture of Bri's devious smile, rejoicing in this outcome and eager to hold his own intimate court with Mia, burned like sea salt in an open wound.

Mia slumped in the seat of her car as the verdict was reported on the radio news. From far away, it seemed, reality slowly set in. She was alone. She would be forced to shift to into an emotionless survival mode or she'd be destroyed by this heartless jungle that respected none and held her innocent man captive. She'd be forced into a reluctant struggle to loosen her heart's dependence on Ty's love, unplugging it from the power source with which he'd lit up her life. Cast back into loneliness, she found herself detouring full circle back to the darkness of being lost and turned out.